MICHELE WALLACE CAMPANELLI

Big Foot

MONSTER
OF THE ICE

Dedication

This book is dedicated to honor God, my late husband Louis V. Campanelli III, David & Greg, Margaret & Tom, Barbara Lossman, Jim Bullard, Jim Pauline, Colette, Ronnie, Roger & Sue, Christopher, Kelsi, Allyson & Nick, the entire Wallace & Campanelli clan, Dawn & Ben Kreiselman, Melisa & Dick, James Cutro, Barbara Koontz, Dr. James N. Jacobson, Sherry MacLean, Mark & Nancy Brasel, Dr. C. Peter Spies, to all those involved in the St. Mark's Church & Choir, Shekinah & HNJ Drama. A very special thank you goes to Fontaine M. Wallace, my wonderful mother and personal editor who taught me to believe in myself and my talents. To God be the glory!

I'd also like to acknowledge Whiskey Creek Press, Debra and Steven Womack, Melanie Ann Billings, Sherry-Derr Wille, Marsha Briscoe, Sloth Dreams Books & Publishing, and Artist Gemini Judson for their great help and publication of this novel.

I sought the Lord, and He answered me,
And delivered me from ALL my fears.

-Psalm 34.4

Table of Contents

DEDICATION..vii

CHAPTER 1 1

CHAPTER 2 5

CHAPTER 3 9

CHAPTER 4 13

CHAPTER 5 17

CHAPTER 6 22

CHAPTER 7..26

CHAPTER 8 29

CHAPTER 9 32

CHAPTER 10 35

CHAPTER 11 38

CHAPTER 12 40

CHAPTER 13 43

CHAPTER 14 46

CHAPTER 15 50

CHAPTER 16 53

CHAPTER 17 56

CHAPTER 18 59

CHAPTER 19 62

CHAPTER 20 65

CHAPTER 21 69

CHAPTER 22 73

CHAPTER 23 77

CHAPTER 24 80

CHAPTER 25 84

CHAPTER 26 86

ABOUT THE AUTHOR 87

Big Foot

MONSTER OF THE ICE

MICHELE WALLACE CAMPANELLI

Chapter 1

Let me begin by introducing myself. My name is Adam Reese, a biologist for Planet X's Wild Kingdom Zoo. I've traveled the world collecting the most ferocious beasts alive to be exhibited in zoos. Some I train. What I'm about to tell you is true.

Regardless of your beliefs in evolution, take a seat, put on a good reading light. What took place on a large desolate island off the coast of Canada will amaze, perhaps even frighten you.

The adventure began with an answering machine message from my estranged wife. "Adam, help! You know I wouldn't ask if it weren't important. Planet X will send a plane. Call Jack to find out what airport. Come now!"

I was pleased to hear from Mary. In retrospect, I should have paid more attention to the resonating fear in her voice. Instead, all my thoughts were hoping she'd decided not to divorce me—that this new project was some excuse for a visit.

The moment I heard from her, I called Jack. He informed me to be on the jet at nine. Jack was supposed to tell Adam which airport, he just said to be at the jet at nine. Jack is our boss. He owns Planet X Zoo and the television studio where my wife films animal documentaries. I'd helped him before training animals for the cameras, but this time things seemed different. I should have gone after Mary alone, but our son wanted to visit his mother. At the time, I didn't think anything about taking him. She'd been gone weeks and, to be honest we were both missing her.

The next day Sean and I arrived at the jet a few minutes early. Grace Landers, another Planet X employee, was waiting in the seat at our right. With her red short hair stuffed underneath a big fur cap, her slender body hidden in overalls, Grace appeared as she always did to me, like a man. Her clothes, her hair, even her job has a masculine flavor-cameraman. I found it odd this time Grace was sent after Mary.

During the flight, I didn't ask Grace why, I just watched my son, Sean, sleeping. All I could think about was how I could break the news to Sean that his mother had asked for a divorce before she left.

Sean looked so innocent with his dark eyes closed, so young at thirteen. Handsome, perfectly proportioned features, a few brown freckles and hair that he bleaches platinum just like his mother; he looked more like Mary than me. For hours on the plane, I watched him dreaming, wondering if I should tell him. It wasn't until we flew over the Canadian island I decided to wait. Glaciers of pale bluish-ice made the giant mass look as if it were built of solid crystals. This beautiful desolate island looked absolutely breathtaking.

Our pilot landed hard near the shoreline, bouncing twice. Bundled up in a blue parka, he jogged to the back of the plane to unload a Snowcat. Enormous tank treads aided this square elevated vehicle out of the plane onto the snow. It looked more like a mini-tank than anything else. When Grace, Sean, and I de-planed, the first thing that struck me was the cold; the zero-chill shot through me, paining my extremities. "Good luck!" The pilot handed me a map and compass. "I'll be back on Monday at nine in the morning." Over the plane's reverberations, I shouted, "Do you know what animal they need my help with?"

"Mary called Jack for the jet, you and an extra cameraman. That's all I know," he shouted to be heard.

My gloved hand shivered as I waved farewell. "Dad, this sucks!"

I turned to my son. Over his thin shoulder was a Cubs gym bag that looked almost too heavy. What he had in it, I could only guess.

"You know how to drive this sucker, Dad?" Sean hopped up next to me in the Snowcat's passenger seat.

"Of course," I answered. The vehicle wasn't exactly like the one I'd driven in the Arctic but the moment I got behind the wheel, it all came back to me: turn on the key, flip the red switch, and hit the gas pedal. Following the compass direction on the map one hundred and fifty degrees northwest, we rattled over the snow to get to the point labeled Polar I. Two long, parallel imprints recorded our tracks in the pressed snow.

In the distance, a round structure faintly rose like a giant turtle shell. It was painted black with, "Polar I" in red letters on the roof. It was hard to miss as we approached. I stopped in front of the massive door. In the middle of icy hills, the building looked alien.

"This must be it." Grace jumped out with her camera bag. "Dad?"

He stopped me from following. "What is it?"

I looked at myself in the rearview mirror. The trip hadn't improved my appearance any. My eyes were lined with bags under them, my facial hair had gotten scruffy, and my face was framed in lacy ice crystals.

"If mom called you here, maybe she wants to work things out."

I moved the mirror back to where it had been. "So, you know?"

"Mom told me. Yeah, I know." He sounded sad and gazed downward.

"Son, I don't want this. I'm going to try to talk some sense into her."

"Don't screw it up, Dad," he pleaded.

I grabbed the door. "Wait here for a second until I tell Mom you wanted to come along."

"She'll be pissed," he warned.

"Stop saying that word. And just wait, okay?"

"Okay."

Slowly I approached the door and knocked. As anxious as I was to clear the air with Mary, I thought it better that I see her first reaction alone, not with our son.

Since no one answered, I opened the door and sauntered in, shaking off the snow from my thick wool parka. In trailed Grace.

"Adam, what happened?" she sputtered.

"Something wrong?" Wiping the cold flakes from my eyes, I saw what looked like blood drops on the desks and the chairs. Papers were scattered over the room, along with broken boxes and filing cabinets. Strewn everywhere lay fallen parkas, lost gloves, and office supplies, as if the entire room had been ransacked in a raid.

Grace rushed from the small galley. "Dead!" she screamed. "There are bodies in pieces in here!"

Human blood? Are those spots actually human blood? I pondered. Suddenly, my heart began pounding with the realization my wife might be in the small kitchen, too. "Mary?"

Grace scrambled to the floor and flipped pages of a reddish-brown spattered book. "Their log is all torn up; I can't read it all."

As she raised the book, some stained pages fell out. "It says Jack put two crews on the island to get footage of several polar bears...one must have gotten in!"

Just then Sean ambled in, his short blond hair popped out from under his hat as the wind knocked it back. His eyes gazed up at the blood-spotted ceiling. His face contorted. "Mom!" he suddenly shouted, "Mom!" as he raced to the galley. I grabbed him in mid-stride.

"Mom!" he was shrieking. Kicking my foot, he broke free and bolted into the galley.

"Noooooooooooooo!" reverberated the blood-curdling scream.

I knew then my wife was dead. No longer feeling the pounding in my head, I surveyed the torn-up, blood splattered room until it began spinning. Grabbing the closest desk, I tried not to pass out.

Chapter 2

I could hardly fathom that Mary was gone. It seemed impossible. How could she have died before we fixed our marriage, before I explained my actions and made things right? I felt as if the whole world came crashing down in an instant. My life would never be the same again—no more happy holidays—no more hearing her prayers at night—never feeling her body pressed against mine or seeing her smile. How could that be?

No matter what our problems, I never wanted harm to come to her.

For a moment, I thought of the first time we'd met. I was working in the zoo and heard a cry of, "Get 'em, Rich." Rich was the fourteen foot alligator leaping below the platform where I held out a dead chicken. Showing the audience how to feed the massive reptile, I was used to hearing "Ahs and Ohs." I immediately turned to see who had spoken.

With straight blonde hair flowing down her back, this gorgeous blue-eyed woman stared back at me. I'd never seen anyone so beautiful. "Watch out!" She suddenly cried out.

With giant jaws gaping below, I dropped the dead chicken into the gator's mouth just before my hand became part of his dinner. My attention immediately flew back to her. With a wink, she started clapping.

"Mom!" Sean tore me from my memory. His arms wrapped around me tightly. "Mom's dead! I saw the blood!"

No, my heart didn't want to hear those words.

Grace tightened her thick blue coat, zipping it back up. "I don't mean to be heartless here, Adam, but we've got to warn the others. They must be somewhere on this island."

"What happened here? How could a polar bear have gotten in?"
I needed to know, pondering the possibilities. Bears tend to head straight for the food source, circling the area, but I remembered there were no tracks appearing near the door. After walking to the door, I opened and examined the frame. No marks, not even one scratch appeared. This is not typical bear behavior I concluded.
"Kevin must have been entering when he was attacked. The body must have been dragged. Look." Grace pointed to the bloodstain trailing from the doorway. "Then the bear stomped into the galley and killed all the others," she surmised. I was struggling with myself. Did I really want to see what was left of my Mary? "Son, Grace is right. We have to warn the others," I finally responded, deciding not to see her battered body. Sean combed his hand through his spiked blond hair. "What about Mom? I don't want to leave her like that?"
"I can't let you stay here alone. We'll come back to make sure your mother's body is taken care of. I promise." Reluctantly, I plodded away from the galley door; I didn't really want to leave her either. Sean trailed after Grace and me into the freezing morning air. I kept checking through the blinding snow for any other signs of a polar bear, fur, blood, nothing but snow appeared as far as I could see.
This didn't make sense. In all my years, every bear I'd ever encountered left evidence. Bears are heavy creatures; a male polar can easily weigh a thousand pounds and yet not even one scratch mark remained at the gory scene. Hurriedly, all three of us climbed into the Snowcat's giant cab and slammed the doors. I turned the key to start the engine. Sean sat closer to me. I noticed he'd left his Cubbies bag. Mary gave him that gym bag last year. He'd never parted with it before. Once he made first baseman of his junior high baseball team, it became his favorite possession.
"Son, your bag?"

"It stays with Mom," he said, choking on his tears.

By leaving it, he was making sure we would soon return, I realized. The Snowcat began rolling across the snow. Through the heavy downfall, we spied a homemade wooden sign reading "Three Polar II." Only three miles to the other film site, I acknowledged, and set my compass straight ahead.

"Dad?"

Words softly came to my lips. "Yes, Son?"

"She would have never come here if you wouldn't have gotten into that fight!" he sputtered between sobs.

Grace interrupted. "Your mother loves working with dangerous animals, Sean. She wouldn't want you to think that way. This was a horrible accident. The bear shouldn't have been able to get inside."

"Shut up! You're probably glad Mom is dead!"

I had to take a deep breath, for this wasn't the time to reprimand him. Soon another domed building became visible, a red inverted bowl half covered in snow. Above the door was a sign: Quest of the Polar Bear, Set II.

"Maybe you should check the place out first," Grace warned.

"Stay here, I'll be right back." I hurried through the blizzard flakes as the cold wind pushed, almost knocking me off my feet. Evidently, this side of the island had worse weather, I surmised.

Getting to the door, I checked the knob. It was locked. A good sign I thought as a wave of relief washed over me. I pounded loudly.

A stocky man flung it open with widened eyes and raised eyebrows on his African-American face. Re-checking our surroundings, I waved to the Snowcat. Grace and Sean jumped out and hurried towards the giant red dome.

"Planet X sent us another cameraman," the man said and smiled. When Grace and Sean were inside, I locked the door and removed my coat. "My name is Adam Reese. I'm a zoologist from Texas. This is Grace Landers; we were sent here by Planet X, and this is my son, Sean."

"Reese? You must be Mary's husband. That was real nice of you to come. I'm Malcom, Malcom Porter." He extended his hand to shake. I quickly shook it, while checking out the interior of the building. The layout looked similar to Polar I, a working area, the galley, and a back room which must be the sleeping quarters. "Where's the rest of your crew?"

Malcom replied, "They'll be back shortly."

He was alone. Fear gripped me. Quickly, I snatched his jacket. "Where are they?"

"With Bret at the lake, getting close-ups of a momma polar bear teaching her cub how to catch a seal." Bret Miller is here? Anger coursed through my body in waves. It was all I could do not to show my growing emotions.

"Miller is on this island?" I finally questioned through clenched teeth.

"Yes," Malcom confirmed.

"We've got to find him," Grace interrupted. "Does Bret have a radio transmitter?"

"In this weather?" Malcom shrugged. "Listen, Reese, I don't know what your problem with Bret is but if you don't take your hands off my jacket, I'm going to screw up your face. Got it?"

Releasing my hold, I quietly announced, "Everyone at Polar I is dead, all of them. We think a polar bear broke in on a rampage, a real man-eater. We've got to warn your team."

Malcom stumbled back. "Is this some kind of joke?"

"No, I wish I were joking, but it's all too real."

"Mary, she's not?" He first looked to me, but I couldn't say the words.

Grace nodded yes. "Please, please, help us locate your crew before it's too late for them too."

Chapter 3

Glancing around Polar II, I noticed a slight difference, three doors not two like Polar I. Peering through them I discovered the room farthest to the right led to a small kitchen. The middle section housed the offices and bunk beds appeared on the left. Nothing appeared askew, but Malcom didn't seem normal to me. He was nervous and fidgety; his eyes never left me. I found myself wondering if perhaps Malcom already knew that those at Polar I were dead before we arrived.

"Did you know what happened back there?" I asked suspiciously. Suddenly Malcom pulled a Glock nine mm gun from underneath his jacket and pointed it straight at Sean. That was the same weapon police used back home, so I quickly recognized the short barrel. But at close range, I knew it could do a lot of damage.

Quickly, I stepped in front of my son. "I'm sorry I grabbed you, Malcom! There's no need for violence."

"You can't go hunt for Bret," Malcom announced. "You don't understand. I wish I could tell you, but I don't know if that's what Bret wants." His eyes darted.

"He knows something," Grace interpreted. She stepped back to stand beside me.

"Do you know what happened to my mom?" Sean asked, peeking out from behind my back. "Please, if you know something, tell me!" Tears again escaped his bright eyes. One rolled down a cheek and dropped onto his dark T-shirt.

"No one wanted anyone to get hurt!" After a tense moment, Malcom finally plopped down the nine mm on a wooden desk, and then he raised both hands to cover his temples in despair. "None of us could have expected this. We would have brought more weapons! Hell! It doesn't matter if I tell you or not. You won't believe me. Nobody will. All that's left of our crew is Bret and me. The rest of both Polar I and II were killed at the lake." He began pacing in a small circle on the packed floor.

"Everyone at Polar II?" Grace trembled, her voice quivering. "You mean your entire crew except Bret and you?"

"Torn to shreds!" Malcom announced as he paused in his steps. His hands flew up. "Bret might be too; he went out to find… where those monsters take the body parts. He wanted to find Al's remains because the director had a satellite phone in his coat, so Bret took off and told me to keep quiet about what happened to the others."

"Tell me what is going on!" I demanded as I edged slowly to the desk, reached it, and gingerly picked up the gun.

Grace followed closely behind me. "Hey, we lost our friends too! Who did this to them?" she said, pleading for an answer.

Malcom shook his head; tears flooded his dark eyes. His large muscular frame shook. In a moment he looked me dead in the eye and claimed, "It's the monster in a white fur coat, a killing machine thirsty for human blood. That's why Mary called Bret and you in, Adam. We needed another cameraman, too, after Saul died, so Mary alerted the company to send Grace. But we knew all along it wasn't for help with the polar bear documentary. We hadn't seen one of those in weeks," Malcom added. "What we found on this island is scarier than anything you can imagine, the greatest discovery of modern man. Mary wanted us all to get credit for the find. She thought Bret could handle it all until you arrived. She was so wrong. The creatures are way too smart. They hunt in packs. Even Bret is probably dead by now." He looked down in despair.

"How long has Bret been missing?" I asked softly, trying to keep the situation calm.

"Since yesterday. But if you search for him, all you'll find is the white fur devil." Malcom buried his head in his hands.

Grace wrapped her arm around Malcom's shoulder. He turned toward her but didn't raise his arms to return the embrace. "Whatever happened, you're not thinking straight," she said. "I remember working with you before. You aren't yourself right now."

"I know I sound crazy. I haven't slept in days but I know what I'm talking about." Malcom pulled away and sat down in front of the black radar screen. The dial hand made one clockwise circle with no bleeps on the screen. He watched for several minutes. "I've got to keep awake and focused. One of them is tagged by a tag gun. They travel together so if I see it, I know where they all are and if they're coming back."

Grace tugged on my sleeve and whispered, "Malcom has obviously gone through a lot, but if he's right about Bret being near the lake, then we should check out if he's dead or not."

I agreed. "Bret can tell us what's really going on," I added.

Grace, Sean, and I moved towards the door. I wasn't sure if Malcom was well enough to be left alone but we really didn't have much of a choice. We had to find that son-of-a-bitch Bret and ask him what the hell was going on. I needed to know what happened to Mary.

"Wait, you can't leave!" Malcom stood as he noticed our change in positions. He catapulted from the chair, stopping only a few feet away. His face tightened; his hands went into fists. "You can't go out there! It's suicide."

"We'll be back as soon as we find Bret."

Malcom reached for the nine mm gun in my hand, but I quickly knocked his hand away. He attempted to take it again but I backed toward the door.

"You don't understand! That weapon and this building are the only protection we have," Malcom said.

"Listen up, we're going to take a look by the lake. If Bret comes, tell him we'll be right back."

"It's getting dark!" His eyes widened in terror.

I tried to speak calmly. "You need rest. Why don't you lie down for a while?"

"Promise me you'll come back," he pleaded, his dim expression deepening the lines around his lips.

I gave a half-hearted smile, realizing Malcom wasn't dangerous—just very frightened. By what, I had no clue. I wondered if perhaps it could have been a giant polar bear or a snow leopard. He did call it "the monster in a white fur coat." Snow Leopards are known for their stealthy way of hunting. They can leap for six feet or more, too, but their smaller feet wouldn't leave such large tracks last night. Perhaps it was a leopard that jumped into Polar I, not leaving much trace. "We'll want the authorities to ask you some questions. Trust me."

"No kidding," Grace said.

"Just tell them everything," Sean added.

Malcom sat back down on the stool, his eyes focusing on the monitor. "It was nice meeting you, Adam and Sean. Lock the door on your way out," he warned. "And leave the gun."

The remark seemed dark, as if he never thought he'd see us again, I thought. I did what he asked and left the gun on the floor. As the three of us trekked through the driven snow towards the Snowcat, the wind caught my breath but did not deaden what I felt inside—heartbroken over Mary.

"Is Malcom going to be all right, Dad?" Sean looked over as he asked me.

"I'm not sure," I said, wondering if any of us would be ever again.

"But we're not spending the night with that lunatic."

"So we won't come back for him?" Sean asked. "We can't just leave him like that, can we?"

"Don't worry, Sean," Grace soothed.

Chapter 4

As the Snowcat headed toward the icy lake, Grace grew quieter.
I immediately wondered why. Was it because she was saddened by the deaths? Perhaps she was afraid for Bret Miller's life? Finding the answers to these questions proved difficult because I couldn't get a read on Bret. Just that name, Bret, started a reel of memories of my wife playing in my head, her body beside mine in bed, her sandy hair fanned over a pillow. Her lips lay inches from mine as she stared back at me with her huge blue eyes shimmering from a small night light in the bathroom. "Do you think we'll last forever?" she had asked in a worried voice.
"Why wouldn't we?"
Her face beamed with a smile. With more enthusiasm than judgment, she answered, saying, "So then you'll never tire of me?"
"Never..." I'd never even given it a second thought as I planted that first kiss.
"Dad, look!"
Interrupting my memories, Sean pointed my attention to what was in the distance. I wiped my eyes, focused my gaze, and spied a small black box in front of the Snowcat. I stopped the vehicle and jumped out to retrieve the case. "Record, Play, Stop, Fast Forward, Rewind," I read buttons on the side. It was a tape player, out in the middle of nowhere. Could this be Bret's, I wondered.
I wiped off the snow from the front of it and pressed down the play switch, raising it to my ear.
"RAAAAARGGGG...RAAAGGGG!" A horrifying noise rang out.
The sound was like nothing I'd ever heard before. I've studied animal

calls since my college days back at Florida State, but this wasn't like anything I'd ever experienced. The sounds sent chills down my spine. They were high pitched like that of a bat, yet rolled like that of a monkey. I hoped Grace had heard this before, so I carried the tape player into the Snowcat and played it for her. Grace's brows raised halfway to her forehead in a panic. "Is the tape eaten?"

I pulled it out and checked; however, the tape was fine. After snapping it closed, I hit play again. It sang like a high-pitched opera singer, only with unrecognizable phrases.

"Do you think it's an animal?" Grace asked. "You're the expert here, Adam."

"I have studied animal calls for years, Grace. Nothing sounds like this. The closest thing might be a mix between a vampire bat with a little rain forest monkey thrown in." I tried to recall any similar animal communication but no sound matched.

"Was there anything else outside?" Sean peered out. "Who could have dropped that? Bret?"

"Could barely see in front of my face," I admitted.

"Look, Dad. There's red! There!" My son pointed.

Through the snowflakes fluttering down against the window, I peered out to where I found the tape player. Sure enough, farther on to the right crimson spotted the snow. Surprised I hadn't seen it out there before, I left the Snowcat again. Trying to see through the blizzard of flakes, I neared the sweater with Florida State University embroidered across the front.

Sean burst out of the vehicle and ran toward the garment as I stood above it. He lowered his hands to grab it, but I quickly warned, "Sean, wait!"

He didn't listen but yanked up the sweater and held it up. There were rips, claw marks right through the center. Even though the sweater was red, the bloodied spots were very apparent.

"Son, give it to me."

"I gave this to Mom for Christmas!" Sean sputtered. "This is Mom's."

"RAAAGHH!"

I checked my hand for the tape player. I must have left it in the Snowcat. Suddenly, my nose was filled with a wretched odor, more potent than a skunk. No, that creature wouldn't live out in the snow. So, what was it?

Sean dropped the sweater. "Dad, what is that smell?"

 "Get back to the Snowcat! Now!"

Not knowing what kind of animal produced such a stench, I pulled him back to the Snowcat. After we climbed in, we slammed the doors. Sean locked his side.

"Dad, what was that stinky smell?"

My fear must have been obvious. "I'm not sure."

Grace reached over me and locked my door. "What's that odor?"

Clunk!

A thud landed on the roof. Grace screamed at a high pitch.

Instantly, I started the engine and hit the gas pedal. Trying to knock it off, I pulled the vehicle both left and right while scratching noises resounded overhead. Moving the mirror latch, I tried adjusting my view to what trounced on top of the Snowcat. Long white fur was hanging over the side.

Sean grabbed the wheel sharply, and the animal yelped as it swished down to the ground next to the vehicle. Again, a wailing cry sent chills down my spine. It wasn't from the cold.

Grace exclaimed, "Can you see what fell?"

Sean asked, "Is it a polar bear?"

Without thinking of the consequences, I pivoted the Snowcat around to face the creature that had just tumbled off. From the new vantage point, I recognized it as a man wearing a white fur coat. His hair was long, curly and blond. Even with his face planted in the snow, I realized who it was. I'd know the bastard, anywhere.

Grace gasped, "It's Bret! Oh, no, we killed Bret!"
Reluctantly, I got out of the Snowcat while Grace ran to the lifeless body. She rolled him over in the snow; his pug nose and the pretty-boy features became apparent. I bent over and checked for a pulse. There was a faint one. Not knowing if that was a good thing or a bad thing, I tossed his limp frame over my shoulder in a fireman's carry.
"I know how you feel about him," Grace announced, "but this isn't the time."
Ignoring her, I moved on, carrying the man I hated most in this world, this cantankerous, mean fool named Bret Miller. He was just too evil to share the same name as one of my favorite beers. What I would do for a drink right now, I thought.
A part of me wanted revenge, enough to leave him out here to die, but my son watched nearby. I might have been tempted if it weren't for my curiosity, the desire to ask an imperative question. I had to know, what happened to my wife?

Chapter 5

Inside the Snowcat, Grace refastened Bret's long fur coat, as he lay sprawled across the seat. Her hands searched his pockets until she unzipped a compartment and pulled out a small, hand-held camera. Quickly, she flipped out the screen and hit the rewind switch.

"Maybe Bret captured something on film." She watched the tiny screen intensely. "Let's see…there's a minute of snow, as if he's running, then nothing. Guess that's it," she reported with a sigh.

Sean took off his hat and put it over Bret's blood-tinged head. "Dad, Bret looks really bad. Is there anything else we should do for him?"

At this moment, did I care if Bret lived or died? That, I wasn't sure of. If I had to pick the one man I wouldn't want to be on a frozen island with, it would be this one. Still, I drove until Polar II came into view. To my surprise, the door was wide open. "Wait here. I'll check on Malcom."

Before I got out of the cab, however, the dark muscular man stepped into the doorway in nothing but a pair of white cotton underwear. In his hand he held a sudsy toothbrush, which he then jammed in his mouth.

"Well, isn't this interesting." Grace smiled, switching on the camera to record. "Maybe we should record his lunacy on tape."

Quickly I shut off the Snowcat and carried Bret in, fireman style.

Sean helped by lifting his trailing legs. Grace followed, continuing to film Malcom as he shut the door after our entry.

"Put on some clothes before you freeze to death," I ordered with a noncommittal smile.

Grace panned the camera closer on Malcom's rear end. She seemed quite taken with the view. "So, tell us about the devil in a white coat again," she interjected.

I laid Bret's body on top of a desk, then stuck my hand in front of Grace's lens. "Stop it, Grace. I think we've been through enough without showing the world a man in his underwear."

"You want me to boogie for you, girl?" Malcom shimmied his hips, then frowned at me. "What's the matter, jealous? You know what they say about us island men."

Trying to contain my anger, to sound as calm and disinterested as possible, I requested, "Dress, please."

Malcom padded down the hall, cooperatively. Picking up the headset of his radio, Sean sat in the chair next to Bret's motionless body. His skin was gaining a better color now, not quite so bluish-gray. Perhaps he'd make it after all, I thought.

"Can you check Bret's pulse?" Grace suggested. "That will look good on the film, as if you are really worried about him."

"Turn off the camera!" I stood up, stiffly. "You're paid to film animals. So far, all we've got is a bunch of dead people and one crazy Islander. No bears, no seals, no whales, not even a damn penguin!"

Malcom returned, wearing socks, a long sweater, and jeans, which hung a few inches from his waist, displaying the top of his briefs. "You want pictures of beasts? All you've got to do is wait. You'll see. Look what one did to Bret here."

I leaned over Bret's body, lowering to his face to see if his breathing had improved. Suddenly Bret's eyes flashed open. The sight of large blue iris made me jump back.

"Where's Mary? Is she okay?" Bret demanded, bolting upright.

Trying not to think about why he should care, I agonizingly retorted, "She's dead."

Horror washed across Bret's face, tears filled in his eyes. For a few minutes, he breathed deeply, then he spoke without hope, saying, "No, no, she can't be...not like the others."

"Who killed my wife?"

"You mean your soon-to-be ex-wife," he shot back.

The reminder cut through me, causing a temporary, deceptive silence. For a few seconds we stared intently at one another.

He calmly continued, saying, "I went down to the lake to see if I could recover Al's body. Our director had a nine mm handgun. Malcom wouldn't go so I went alone." Bret patted his jacket. "Where's my camera? I think I caught one on tape."

"I rewound it but there's nothing but snow," Grace informed, looking aghast. "What do you mean caught one?"

"Damn, it ran too fast." Bret pulled his long blond hair back into a ponytail with a rubber band. "I saw your Snowcat in the distance, but it must have hit me from behind."

"What hit you?" she asked.

Bret tightened his hair band. Then he felt around and said, "Here on the back of my head. There's a bump."

"A polar bear attacked?" Sean questioned, with an eagerness in his voice.

"I don't think a bear could have smacked me like that. It felt like something hard... maybe a rock."

Examining his head, I felt around but only found a small bump.

"Impossible! Polar bears attack the back of your head or neck with their teeth. You haven't got one cut from a claw or even one tooth mark. This doesn't look like any bear attack I've ever read about," I said, thinking over my classes in college. Then I remembered the polar bears live chickens. They always bit the neck immediately or swatted them down. Any bear, even a baby, would have left a lot more damage than this, even if it had been only toying with Bret. Polar bears are known for playing with their prey first, but even one strike would have left near fatal damage from blood loss.

Grace leaned down, moved Bret's blond hair, then panned for a close up of Bret's small crimson bump.

"Are you getting this?" Bret inquired.

"Yes, but if it wasn't a bear, what did this to you?" Grace questioned, more for the camera than for her own curiosity.

Bret glanced up with widened eyes, portraying a horror I had never seen before in him. Then his mouth spoke this unforgettable word, "Bigfoot."

"First, we have a devil in a white fur coat, and now Bigfoot! Have you and Malcolm both gone mad?" Grace put down the camera and smiled. "This is a joke, right?"

"Maybe it's the bump on your head causing you to think you saw something like Bigfoot," I said. "There is no such thing, Bret. No cadavers have ever been discovered where footprints have been cast. They always turn up to be done by local pranksters or hicks wearing monkey suits. Believe me, if there were such a creature, I would have trapped one. That would fulfill my life's mission to prove to the world that the creature exists."

"Oh, that's a good line," Grace interjected.

"Oh, you're wrong. Bigfoot, Yeti, Abominable Snowman, whatever you want to call it, it's alive and it has killed our team. I for one am not going to jail for any murder! No one is going to believe us unless we at least get it on film." Bret shivered from more than the cold. "Will you help me, Grace? You're the best videographer Planet X has. I don't think it's possible to trap one, even with Mr. Bigshot over here."

Beep, beep sounded from the monitor.

Malcom rushed over to sit back down in front of the screen where a shiny yellow blip approached from the corner. Malcom started groaning, "Ohhhhhhh... one's coming back."

"Is the door locked?" Grace asked Sean, panic forcing her eyebrows to her hairline.

My son quickly went to the door, checked the lock with a shaky hand, and announced, "Yes."

"No matter how scared you are, Grace, film it!" Bret ordered her, rising shakily to his feet in anticipation. "We'll need proof of their existence."

Not knowing what to expect, I listened intently. There was no sound, but that horrid smell suddenly returned. Again, the stench burned my nostrils.

"They're not far now," Bret said. "Smell that?"

"Who could miss it?" My hand covered my nose.

"I've got my equipment in the back of the Snowcat, everything we'll need, lights, cameras, generators," Grace informed.

"You'll have to get it later." Bret pulled back a stray blond lock behind his ear so he could see. "You don't want to be outside when one gets close. Next time we'll film it together, from different angles."

Hearing the blips gaining speed, Malcom watched the little yellow dot growing closer and said in horror, "There isn't going to be a next time. Three meters, two... one!"

Bam! The walls vibrated from such a tremendous blow that I could only conclude that something very heavy just landed hard on the roof. What creature could jump that high or weigh that much? A polar bear can weigh over a ton, easily, and they've also been known to jump twelve feet, I recalled. To make the building shake like this, one must weigh over two tons, probably a male bear the size of a small truck. The entire building rattled again as if it had collided with a great force.

"Dad!" My son ran to me and huddled behind my back. Bam!

Grace raised the camera to her eye and slowly approached the small window. Nearly immediately, she dropped the equipment and let out a blood-curdling scream. "My God! What the hell is that? What is that?" she asked in a tremulous voice.

Chapter 6

While Grace continued to scream, Bret snatched the camera off the floor, swung it onto his shoulder, and darted to the window. Wanting to know what they were seeing, I drew closer, peering through the window to glimpse what had scared Grace.

Bam! The walls again reverberated, this time near the galley. The rattling continued for several more minutes. A framed picture popped off the wall and shattered glass over the floor.

"What is doing that, Dad?" Sean screamed.

From underneath the window, a wooly mass of thick, long, white hair rose. The ape-like features stared back at me, its red-pupil eyes shined angrily, almost human in response. Screeching with a high-pitched roar, the beast revealed elongated incisors in its gaping mouth.

I tried to catch my breath, but what was before me was something straight from the bowels of hell. Only the devil could have molded a monster so horrifying. I repulsed instinctively.

Bret backed away, the camera dropping from his shoulder to his side. He breathed in and out deeply, transfixed at the unwelcome discovery. "It can't be," he muttered.

The creature then cocked his head as if to say, "You should be scared." Then it stepped out of view from the window with two mighty crunching noises.

"Son, stay away from the window!" I demanded, wanting to shield my son from the nightmare.

Bam! Another blow banged the entrance, forcing a bulge in the solid steel door.

Bam! It repeated the move, causing a larger dent.

"Can it get in?" Sean questioned, fearfully scurrying to my side.

"Get behind me!" I bolted to the desk and shuffled through papers, looking for any type of weapon at all, even a letter opener. I questioned Malcom, saying, "Where are the kitchen knives?"

"Don't know," he answered.

"What did you do with them?" I grabbed Malcom by his sweater.

Then as quickly as the banging noises had begun, they stopped. After a moment I checked both windows, but there was nothing but blowing snow and a set of very large footprints now quickly disappearing in the drift. Waiting, I wanted to be sure what we had seen wasn't coming back. "Oh no," were the only words I could speak.

"Dad, what did you see?"

From the area in front of the base, sounded a muffled tearing like ripping metal. Immediately, I remembered the only thing outside, our only means of transportation. I ran to the door, but I couldn't seem to muster the strength to unlatch the lock.

"Don't open it!" cried Bret.

"But it's destroying the Snowcat!" My hands suddenly trembled over the latch. "Dad, don't open the door!" warned Sean.

And there I stood, with my hand over the lock, too frightened to move, quivering like a child. My mind reeled in disbelief at what I saw just moments before, a living creature, inches away, glaring at me with monstrous eyes through snow-frosted pane. The four inch thick clear plastic had been the only thing saving my life and the others.

The ripping and bending metal sounds stopped. All turned silent for quite some time, except for the pounding of my heart. My shaking fingers slowly twisted the dead bolt and opened the door a few inches. I peered out with one eye.

Before me was no longer a mighty Snowcat. Now its shiny doors were ripped from its hinges. The engine lay scattered in pieces across the snow, oozing oil and gasoline. The tank's wheel tracks were torn off and thrown over a hundred feet away.

"Shut the door," Bret ordered. "It's damaged beyond repair."

I closed it and turned the bolt lock back for security. Grace, Bret, and Sean stood huddling near me. Their terrified faces matched mine.

Grace hugged herself as she openly wept. "Now we have no way out of here!"

I up righted a desk chair, suddenly feeling the need to sit before I fell over. My brain felt as if I had been shot with a loaded pistol. It took me nearly a minute to find the courage to announce, "We'll find another way."

"What animal could have done that with its bare hands?" Sean asked timidly. For the life of me, I couldn't pronounce the name. It didn't seem possible.

Grace finally responded, "It was Bigfoot, Sean."

"Are you joking?" my son softly asked.

"We're not on candid camera, Boy," said Malcom. He then held out his arms, making an ape-like noise.

Out of frustration I responded, "There's got to be another explanation. It can't be possible that there is such a beast. It surely would have been discovered long before now."

"Bigfoot ruined our only way of escaping, Adam. It knew what to do to keep us prisoners. And that's exactly what we are, mice in a giant cage." Bret wiped the sweat off his forehead, proving how terrified he was in this Artic weather. "Do you think a polar bear would have done that, Adam? You're the expert here. It seemed deliberate to me, even intelligent, as if it knew this door was a way to get in. That's why it kept pounding on it. It's far smarter than anything we've ever encountered before, right?"

I just couldn't fathom the beast was real. Closing my eyes, I tried to convince myself with weak statements. "There's no such thing as Bigfoot. No one has ever captured, contained, or even found a corpse of one."

Suddenly Grace blurted out, "There was a creature documented in the Himalayas, similar to this Bigfoot, only short-haired, that lived in the snowy mountains."

"And aliens landed in Mexico." I shook my head, protesting vehemently. "Gray with big eyes and three large fingers, right? Believe me, if they were real, I would have trapped one by now and stuck it in Planet X's zoo to make Jack a fortune."

Grace continued to weep softly. A part of me wanted to do the same thing. Perhaps I would have if Sean had not been standing beside me. It was my fault for getting him into this mess in the first place. Now his mother was dead... I took a few moments recalling our loss and knew I needed to stay strong for Sean. At this point I'm all he has. "We will wait until the authorities come. Jack will realize we're all missing and he'll send help for us soon. In the worst case scenario, the plane will return on Monday to pick us up."

"Yeah, and they'll think we killed both crews when the investigators get here!" Bret reminded sharply.

"No one will believe we could have done that to the Snowcat," I said, coming right to the point. "No human could have done that. This one has the strength of ten men. You and I together could not have ripped the Snowcat tracks off and carried them so far."

Chapter 7

"I have tracked hundreds of different animals across every continent," Bret commented as he peered through the window over the snow, which was brightened by dazzling moonlight. With an inscrutable gleam in his eyes and a wicked crocodile grin he questioned, "You're a zoologist, Adam. Do you think, together, we could trap this thing?"

Sean lowered himself to sit on top of the desk. He crossed his arms and argued, "Dad, this isn't a video game; these monsters are real."

"Planet X doesn't have a license to trap anything on this island," Grace added, her fine-boned face reflecting wariness.

Bret spoke without compunction, saying, "I think the authorities will understand why we took matters into our own hands."

"We should film the creature until help arrives." Grace glanced at me gravely. It was clear she didn't want me to risk capturing it.

"Do Adam or I look like Sly Stallone?" Bret asked, trying not to laugh. "This isn't the movies. That creature is out there, and it wants us dead. We can't just film the thing. Look at the door! We need to trap it or we're all going to die locked in here."

Grace took a few deep breaths, then mustered the courage to respond.

"Try not to be so blunt, in front of the boy," she said and nodded toward Sean.

"Tranquilizers can prove too dangerous." I remembered a huge, silver back gorilla in Africa who almost ripped my head off before the medication took effect. "We may have no other choice but to destroy it."

"That's a man's answer to everything," Grace protested. "Shoot or kill."

"Do you have a better idea?" I came straight to the point, knowing options were limited.

"If it's our missing link, then we have an obligation to protect the greatest discovery of our lifetime!" Grace reminded enthusiastically. "I'll retrieve one of my lenses from what remains of the Snowcat, film it, and wait until the authorities come. Let the authorities see that creature on tape."

I paced to the door and fingered the indentations the beast punched in it. Six inches deep, they protruded into the room. Next to it was a small hole near the latch. One more strike and the large animal would have broken the lock. "This door won't hold much longer," I announced.

Grace leaned over and snatched the tape recorder from out of my jacket pocket. "There may be some kind of clue on this that might help us understand this animal's behavior better."

The tape began to play. First the beast screeched, then the voice of my dead wife resounded, "Polar II, this is Mary Reese. Polar I is under attack... it's" Then there was a blood curdling scream.

Sean cringed. That horrified cry sent chills down my spine. Poor Mary, I never would have wished such a death on her, even in the darkest nightmares. "Stop playing that, Grace!"

Bret reached to hit the stop button, then placed the tape player next to the dark monitor. "Nothing recorded can save us." He turned to Malcolm and said, "But you have something that can. Where's Al's gun?" Bret pointedly asked him. "It wasn't on the director's corpse which means he must have left it here."

"Chucked it into the snow, Man. This dude already tried to hurt me and the bullets were missing," Malcolm retorted. "As far as I'm concerned, you guys are as untrustworthy as that uglier, hairier white thing out there."

"You tossed out our only chance of survival!" Bret spelled it out for him, venomously. "I had bullets."

Sean suddenly got up and walked into the hallway before the galley.

"Please don't talk that way in front of my son," I said to Bret, and moved after him. "Bret didn't mean we were really going to die, Son." Before I could reach the hall, Sean returned with an ax. "We can use this, Dad, to break up the desks, board up the window and door." Slowly, he lifted the tool above his head and rammed it down onto the farthest desk. The desk shattered into several pieces. Sean picked up the largest piece of wood and walked towards one of the windows, and then he wedged it in to cover half the window. "This can work!" he added triumphantly.

"There any nails around here?" I asked Malcolm.

"There might be some on that shelf," Bret replied for him, and then pivoted to Sean, taking the ax away. "Help me finish breaking up the desk, Kid."

Reaching up, I got on tiptoes to flip open the lid of a shoebox. Inside sat a small hammer and about a dozen four-inch nails. "Would these be long enough?" I wondered aloud.

A beep sounded at that moment. Glancing down at the screen, I saw a dot blinking to the right of the building.

"It's coming back," Malcom announced ominously.

Grace screamed, "No!"

Wham! Faster than lightening, two massive white hairy arms crashed through the window and encircled my son, ripping him off the floor. Sean screamed in terror.

I ran to the window. By the time I had reached the opening, there was nothing, but snowflakes and wind punctuated with echoing cries of, "Dad! Help! Dad!" The board, which had been in my son's hands, lay rocking on the floor.

Chapter 8

"Going after your son is suicide!" Grace blocked in my path as I grabbed the ax from Bret. I pushed her aside, unlocked the door, and ran around the building. Underneath the broken window large footprints appeared. My eyes followed them till I saw the creature was running with Sean draped over his shoulders.

"Adam, don't!" Grace cried out.

No matter where the creature traveled, there wasn't a chance in hell I would not go after my son. My boots trekked behind the huge snow prints.

Suddenly, a screech pierced the wind. In all my years of studying wildlife, I had never heard such an erratic area of octave ranges, like unrecognizable opera. Brushing the snowflakes from my eyes, I spied the white furry mass begin to scale the face of a mountain. It jumped several boulders before reaching a cave twenty feet above.

"Hold on, Son!" Praying my son wouldn't be dropped, I grasped a large rock, pulling myself to the top. I realized the creature was bigger yet more agile than I. On the second jump, I grabbed the boulder and slowly lifted myself to lie on top of it. Two more, I counted, and then I'd be at the ledge of the cave.

I kept my gaze on the entrance as I leaped for the third rock. Grasping the ledge, I pulled myself to the top. Unexpectedly, the ax dropped from the crook of my elbow and tumbled down, landing at Bret's feet.

Surprised Bret had followed, I shouted, "What the hell are you doing here?"

"Trying to save your butt!" he retorted as he zipped up the ax in his jacket then climbed. When Bret reached my level, the third rock, he cupped his hands. "I'll lift you. You'll make it with a boost."

With no choice but to trust him, I placed my foot in Bret's hands and bolstered myself onto the ledge. I rolled over it, then reached down to help him to my level.

The moment he stood beside me, I turned to peer into the cave. I could also hear something breathing, deep and heavy, as I gazed at a distant light.

After Bret unzipped his coat, he handed me the ax. "Take it!" My hand flew to signal hush. "Let's do this quietly," I whispered.

Warily, we entered the cave. On the walls red outlines depicted

animals. Bret pulled out a small, handheld camera and clicked several pictures while the flash lit up the illustrations.

"I found this camera outside of the Snowcat. There was a lens too for the handheld, but this digital one is too bright in here—gives us away," he whispered. He shoved the camera back into his pocket before I could reprimand.

Suddenly a boy's scream resounded through the cavern. I instinctively ran toward the light ahead and burst into a room. Wooden bowls on top of a strange- shaped table became visible. In the corner, smoke curled up from a small fire to an endless ceiling.

Bret caught up, gasping. "Can you see him?" Thud!

We whirled toward the noise from a crevice on the right. My son hung by his feet, tied with hide ropes. He was banging on the walls with his fists.

Ecstatic to find Sean alive, I stretched upward to grab him. Bret

jumped to untie my son. "I can't reach him."

I lifted the ax and swung hard through the rope nearly beyond my

reach. Released, Sean dropped into my now outstretched arms. I gently lowered him to the floor, checking him. "You okay?"

Sean grimaced. "Bigfoot smells awful."

"I don't need to find out." I smiled. "Let's go."

Quickly the three of us rushed back through the dark cavern, feeling our way along the walls. Ahead of us streamed light, then an entrance framed drifting snowflakes. In an instant, we lowered ourselves to the sea of white below.

In only a few seconds a howl resounded from above.

From the entrance of the cave, a giant white mass jumped angrily.

"Run!" I screamed horrified. "Run!"

Chapter 9

With dark, lifeless eyes and long fanged teeth, more white beasts burst out from the cave. Their body hair fluttered in the wind, almost camouflaging them in the falling snow. I could barely believe my eyes. This sight was a nightmare. "Dad!"
Another creature was running over the hill to their right. I grabbed my son's arm and started to run. Bret zoomed ahead of us. In the far distance lay Polar II. Without looking back, Bret reached the door first and banged his fist. "Open up! It's us!" The door flew open and Bret ran in then turned around. Horror washed across his face at the scene. I was glancing back at the creatures closing in on my son and me.
One even stretched out his arm to reach Sean. Running, as I never had before, I snatched Sean up and bolted inside Polar II. Quickly, Bret slammed the door.
Bam!
The creatures banged on the door. Screeching noises resounded from every direction. I whirled around and took in a deep breath, trying to calm myself. They were outside, all of them, beating on the walls. They couldn't get in; or could they? His eyes flew to the broken window and door. Reddish black eyes were peering in through two wooden boards Malcom or Grace must have nailed up.
Bam! Bam! Bam! Bam! Grace screamed. "Go away!"
Sean sat up, staring at me, his face contorted with fear.

Was this it? I wondered. Have our deaths come in the shape of white furry masses? I'd spent my whole life trying to save endangered species, trying to educate the public on causes that really matter. Now the most amazing discovery, the man- beast, might cost us our very lives. "Dad?" Sean's eyes were tearing.

I wrapped my arms around my son. "They can't get in."

The scratching grew more intense, accompanied with their weird calls and much heavy grunting. Grace held her hands to her ears, closing her eyes, trying to shut them out. I walked past the window and saw the creature still at the boards, trying to knock them down. One creature leaned into a crack. His white, furry face was three inches from mine. Only a thick piece of glass lay between the boards. "You'll have to do better than that," I challenged.

The haunting eyes squinted, as if trying to understand.

"By the time I get through with you, I'll have your head mounted on my wall. I used to hate seeing animals like that, but not now, not this time. I'll have your cheeks stuffed like a pig's and lay your fur before my fireplace by next winter's first night," I continued forcefully.

"What the hell's the matter with you?" Bret roared. "That's the greatest discovery on earth!"

"Don't lecture me," I snipped. My cold breath was causing the pane of the glass to whiten. "You of all people have no room to talk about morality." Grace walked toward the window, then reported, "It's still watching our every move."

The creature held out a furry hand and pressed it up against what was left of the windowpane. Grace slowly lifted her hand and laid it against the glass. It slowly moved a finger.

Grace's index followed. "Don't kill us. Please, don't kill us."

The creature shut its fanged mouth, then turned away. One by one, the others quietly followed, all disappearing over the snowy hill.

Chapter 10

"On our arrival at Polar II, Jack called, complaining we were already
a day late shooting the surroundings. The Snowcat that dropped us off
had a satellite cell phone in the glove box. Did yours?" Bret suddenly
asked me.
"If there was one inside, I didn't see it."
"Maybe someone should check the wreckage," Grace added.
Malcom glanced at the monitor. "It's clear for suicide."
Sean grimaced.
I took my son's head in my hands, his wet, spiky blond hair sticking to
my fingers. "I'll be right back," I said, then walked to the door and
unlatched it.
"Dad!"
"If you see anything on that screen, Malcom, you scream bloody
murder until I hear you."
Bret opened the door. "Make it quick!"
Out in the cold air, I couldn't see much. It was a race against the clock,
I knew. I had to search the debris before darkness set in. If the
Yeti didn't see me, a polar bear might.
In a study, my wife conducted on the feeding habits of polar bears
years ago, I remembered learning that polar bears could smell flesh for
miles, see through icy water, and feast until dawn. Their incisors could
kill a man with one bite. With food shortages, what else would make
a perfect meal but a man?

In front of me lay what was left of the Snowcat. The wheels were ripped off. The doors and windows had been broken off and the engine lay sprawled across the snow in a scattered array of shiny metal.

Hurdling over the parts, I finally grabbed at a part of the door. Easily, it fell. The heavy door had had its hinges ripped off by a creature with the strength of ten men.

Climbing into the passenger's seat, the tank teetered over to one side. I braced myself for the tumble, but it swayed only twice.

Slowly, I leaned in and began searching, opening the glove compartment. Inside was an orange box. A sigh of relief escaped my mouth in a puff of cold air. "Please be a phone."

With a slip of the clasp, the box clicked open. At the bottom lay a cell phone with a satellite tracking antenna and a flare gun. A smile crossed my face. A possible weapon! Not as good as the one Malcom had thrown into the snow but a gun, nevertheless. Quickly, I checked but saw only one flare. Good. Immediately, I loaded and tucked the gun into my jacket. This gun no one would know about.

My shaky fingers dialed Planet X's phone number. Barely able to hear over the wind, I cupped my hand over one ear and leaned in.

"Jack Sigman's office."

"I need to speak to Mr. Sigman."

"Hello? Is anyone there?"

"Put Sigman on the phone!" I screamed.

"I can't hear you. We have a bad connection. Call back, please." She hung up. "Damn!" Picturing the blonde-haired floozy that bounced around Jack Sigman's office, my face wrinkled in disgust. She'd already broken up two marriages and was now working on Jack's. She was pretty all right, like a red, yellow, and black coral snake, attractive, but poisonous.

I redialed the number.

"Hello?" The same female voice answered.

I screamed loudly. "This is Adam Reese! Can you hear me?"

"Adam is that you?" she asked.

"Put Sigman on the phone! Now!"

"You don't have to scream," she said. "I'll put you right through."

"Hello." A deep voice came on the line. "Adam?"

"The crew is dead. We found something. You're not going to believe it!"

After a long pause, Jack inquired, "Have you been drinking?"

"There's something after us! Send the plane to the island now or we're all going to die!"

"What's after you? What's happened? Is Mary all right?"

"She's dead. Both crews are dead," I announced coldly. "Now send a rescue plane!"

"Adam, what did you do to Mary?"

 "Send the plane!"

"All right, but if you harmed one hair on Mary's head..." Fighting back tears, I had to hang up.

Chapter 11

Quickly, I returned. Before I even had time to shake the snow from my shoulders, Bret unlocked the door of Polar II.

"Did you find a satellite phone?" he asked.

"Yes, I called Jack. He's sending a rescue plane."

"Yahoo," Grace cheered. "We're getting out of here!"

I took a seat and placed my coat on top of the desk, making sure no one could see the flare gun tucked inside. "I suggest we work together and gather hair or foot molds from around the building."

Bret went to the camera and rewound the tape. He sat transformed for some time watching, and then said, "There have been so many pictures taken already. The only way we can prove to the world that we aren't killers or liars is to catch one." Bret turned and looked me in the eye. "Remember our African Safari back in 1999. We trapped a four-hundred-pound lion."

"We did that with good intentions."

"We released that lion miles away and it came back. Seven villagers were killed and Planet X is still paying off the lawsuits. Don't act like someone didn't get rich off of our actions then. This time it could benefit us financially and prove all of us innocent of murdering all these people. Otherwise, no one will think we are telling the truth."

"I can't believe what I'm hearing." Grace gasped.

"What's wrong with clearing our name and making a buck in the process?" Bret asked.

"Nothing if you're a poacher," Grace snipped.

"The only safe way is to bring one back dead," I concluded.

Sean looked between the boards on the window. He stood transfixed on something that was catching his attention. "Dad," he called.

"Get away from the window, Son."

"Dad, out there. Look." Sean pointed.

I hurried over, peering into a tiny crack through the wooden beams. Instead of another massive scary beast, I saw a smaller one sniffing and scratching at the snow.

Bret moved in behind me, peering over my shoulder. "We could build a small cage and bring back that baby one."

Suddenly, the little creature dug deeper and dove into a hole. Grace stared out the window. "Are you sure that was an infant?"

"It could have been a polar bear cub," I realized. "I'll go to the galley and get some food from the fridge. If we can draw it out maybe we can see what it is."

"How come no blip showed on the monitor," Bret wondered.

"It picks up only large animals," Malcom informed.

Sean's face suddenly turned pale. "Dad, are you sure you want to open the galley door?"

It took all my strength to even touch the doorknob. I took a deep breath, remembering all the blood and body parts at Polar I. Not looking down, I opened the door and hurried to the fridge. Inside were hamburgers on a plate, ready to be cooked.

My mind flashed back to the last time Mary and I threw a barbeque. Drinking, leaning over the flames, Mary asked me to let Bret cook instead. I shoved her back and told everyone, "I want a divorce, you bitch! Stop telling me what to do!" Mary tossed down her apron and walked out for the last time.

Grief suddenly overtook me. What a jerk I had been! I had to take a few deep breaths. Then I grabbed the plate of burgers. Tripping over something, I didn't dare glance down to see what it was as I hurried out of the room.

Chapter 12

Breaking down the wooden cabinets, I used the ax and with remaining nails built a box with one end open. Needing hinges, I removed the anchors from the galley's door. I left the door leaning against the opening, not wanting to leave any bloody view. It didn't take long to anchor a flap of wood to the box's front. With a thin piece of wood, I wrapped wire at the bottom and created a middle trip wire.

Testing it out, I set open the door, propped open the flap with the thin wood stand, walked away and yanked the trip wire. Wham! The door fell down. My lips curled into a smile.

"That might actually work," Bret said.

Quickly, I went to the box and attempted to raise it. I could only slightly move one end before it came crashing back down. "I can't."

Sean volunteered, "I'll help, Dad."

"We'll need everyone to lend a hand, even you, Malcom. Son, I want you to watch the screen and if you see anything holler as loud as you can."

"Great," Bret said, sarcastically. "All our lives up to one kid's attention span."

"Are you going to help or just sit there and be a pain in the ass?" I asked.

"I'll get one end," Grace said.

Malcom laid the hamburger plate inside the box. Grace, Malcom, and I each grabbed a side, then Bret came and slowly the four of us lifted the heavy cage.

My son opened the front door. Through the wind, he yelled, "Don't worry. I'll watch the monitor."

My muscles began to shake carrying the homemade contraption. I don't know how we managed but we carried the heavy contraption about a hundred yards. "This will do."

We lowered the trap to the snow. Bret checked that the hamburger meat was all the way in the back. Then he quickly propped open the door. "It's set. Let's go," he yelled.

"We should bury it a bit." Grace pushed snow up the sides of the cage. Disguising the cage would help our chances of working, I realized.

I began lifting snow and plopping it on the cage's roof. When it was covered, I skimmed a light layer of snow even over the door to camouflage that as well.

"It looks more like a cave than a trap," Grace commented.

"With an easy meal," I agreed.

The door to Polar II suddenly flew open and my son screamed, "They're coming!"

I lifted my head just in time to see movement in the snow in the north. The fur was reflecting a different shade of white in the dull sunlight. "Run!"

The four of us rushed toward Polar II. Immediately, Malcom slammed the door behind us, quickly locking it. We looked out the window at the creatures coming toward the cage. Bret grabbed the handheld camera. He put it between the crack of the boards on the window and his eye.

I gave him a look like, "not now," but deep inside I knew Bret was right. Any station would pay millions for footage like this. And if they were lucky to bring one back alive, it would mean he'd never have to work again a day in his life.

Suddenly three furry creatures swarmed the homemade trap, encircling it, studying. One peered inside. After making screeching noises, two of the beasts held up the trap door as the third leaned down and pulled out the hamburger plate with one hand.

Bret gasped.

The creature held the plate high above his head. Then the three shrilled, "AAAAAARGH!"

The noise sent chills down my spine. "How long did that take them to figure it out?"

"Not thirty seconds," Grace said, aghast.

Bret waited until the creatures ran away and lowered the camera. "We'll have to make a new kind of trap. One they won't see coming and with a different kind of bait."

I remembered how we led the lion over a trap while it had been hunting its meal. I knew exactly the kind of trap Bret meant. I cringed. "You mean one of us as bait."

Chapter 13

"Are you up to the challenge, Adam?" Bret asked.

"To use live bait is ridiculous! We'll wait here until the rescue plane comes then we'll take the film we've got to Jack at Planet X," Grace said.

"I'm not giving up this film for less than a million," Bret stated.

"Planet X owns the film," Grace reminded. "Didn't you sign the agreement like I did? Anything we capture becomes the sole property of Planet X."

"Then we won't tell them," Bret said. "We'll say that after we found the others we were too afraid to film. Then we'll take our proof and sell it to the tabloids."

Wham!

A chair broke, halfway across the room. I looked up and realized my son threw it. His eyes were filled with rage.

"Son?"

"My mother is dead because of those things out there. Now you want to kill my father too! All you care about is dollar signs! My Dad was right about you, Bret. You are an ass."

I walked over to my son and embraced him. "Son, don't."

"Why not; it's the truth?"

"Hey, Kid, I risked my neck to make sure you came out of that cave alive!"

"Dad, let's just get out of here."

"The fate of the world rest on our hands, Kid," Bret said.

"What?" Sean asked.

"Don't you see? If these things are what they are, they'll change everything. They'll change the history books in your schools."

Sean broke out of his Dad's arms. "It sounds like you think my Mom's life is nothing more than a money ticket."

Bret raised his hand. "I won't dignify that with an answer."

Sean pressed. "Dad, when I was in the cave. I thought I heard a woman's voice calling out. At the time, I thought it was just the wind, but what if Mom's not dead? What if she's still trapped in the cave somewhere?"

For a moment, I clung to the hope Mary could still be alive. And then I remembered. "We found her red sweater with blood all over it."

"It was away from all the other bodies, Dad, in the snow!"

"No more talk about live bait. Maybe we should all get some sleep." Grace went to the few remaining cabinets, found blankets, and tossed them to each person. Bending down, she pulled out some pillows from the lowest shelf. "This will help him rest."

"How can you even think of sleeping?" Bret asked.

"I'll take first watch. Every couple of hours we'll switch." I looked down at the watch on my wrist. "At two, I'll wake you. Then, Malcom, we'll take five to nine. Agreed?"

The men nodded one by one. "But, Dad?"

Quickly, I laid out a blanket and a pillow. "Here you go, Son."

Slowly, Sean made a place beside him and curled up. I watched for a few moments, the shaking of his shoulders, the way he turned away his head. I knew he was mourning the loss of his mother. I could only hope it wouldn't take its toll.

"Dad," Sean whimpered. "Do you think it's possible Mom's still alive? All I saw was blood."

"I want to believe."

"Don't you love her anymore?" Sean asked.

It didn't take me long to answer. "I'll always love your mother."

Sean's shoulders stopped trembling and before long, I watched him drifting off to sleep, hearing one last sentence come from his lips. "I miss her too, Dad."

Chapter 14

My watch went by smoothly. When it was Bret's turn to guard, I must have fallen asleep because I awoke with Malcom shaking my shoulders.

"Adam!"

Quickly, I checked on my son sleeping beside me, then rose and went to the window where Malcom stood.

He pointed down through the cracks in the window boards with a frightened look on his face. "They're digging."

"Why didn't you wake me when they appeared on the monitor?"

Underneath the window several massive white creatures were scratching at the snow, creating a giant hole under Polar II.

Bret came up behind me, wiping his eyes. "What's going on?"

I went to the floor and peered through the wood to a thin layer of steel. "We're protected."

"That's what I thought," Malcom said. "They can't get in that way, right?"

Wham! The wood blew up in the middle of the floor. Shards shot out in every direction. Sean jumped awake.

Grace screamed. "What the hell?"

Wham!

A white fist broke through the buckling metal. Sharp-clawed fingers grasped around the hole at anything which might be close by. I picked up the ax and swung. Just as the ax whirled, the creature's hands lowered.

Bret snatched his coat. "We have to leave."

We looked at each other; four more arms burst in through the metal. The wood broke beneath our feet, the hole growing large enough for one of them to fit through.

"Not out there!" Grace said.

"I know a place." Bret grabbed the camera. "It's near the lake. Come on. They can't see us leave."

As a group, we hurried from Polar II. The wind felt colder than before, stinging my face. I pulled my son close and glanced back. The window boards were being ripped off. Behind the broken glass six of the white furry beasts stared back.

"Hurry! It's not far now." Bret said.

We ran as fast as we could over the ridge. From here, I could see the frozen lake in the distance and hear the strange vocals of the animals in pursuit. The snow grew deeper and the travel got harder. My son was having the most difficult time keeping up. Finally I gained the courage to glance back. Five of the creatures were following, at speeds double our own, their massive feet giving them advantage.

Suddenly Bret reached the edge of the frozen water. He began skidding. "Come on!"

Putting my boot on the lake, I wondered if there were any weak spots. Ignoring the danger, fearing being eaten over falling into the frozen lake, I hurried after Bret and the others across the smooth surface, half slipping, half running.

The creatures stepped on the edge, touching the icy lake and testing its strength. A beast leaned over and punched the ice, easily breaking through. Then a horrible shattering sound began as the ice cracked in long outstretching lines.

"Spread out our weight. Quick!" Bret said.

Suddenly, Malcom fell through the ice with a giant splash. "Malcom!" Sean yelled.

"Keep going! I'll get him!" Immediately, I lowered myself over the edge of the water, trying to grab Malcom's hand. As I peered through the freezing hole, what I discovered terrorized me. Malcom's eyes were bulging in horror as a large female polar bear bit his neck and dragged him down into the crystal depths. Blood oozed to the surface in a giant pool of crimson.

The group was far ahead now. White Bigfoot creatures raced around the lake to trap us on the other side. If I was going to live, I had to catch up to them before the creatures. Trying not to think of Malcom's fate, I rose and ran like hell.

Ahead of me, Bret dropped near the snowbank and dug, revealing a steal sub's hatch. He flipped the round door open. Grace lowered herself, Sean, and then Bret. Smelling the stench of the beasts closing in, I grabbed hold of the ladder with the crook of my elbow and leaped. Bret slammed the door shut and locked it by turning the wheel from inside.

Wham! Wham! The pounding of the animal's fist went against the latch. I tried to hold on to the ladder. The force of the jump hurt my arm and I dropped several feet to the steel floor. As I rolled downward, my shoulder hit the back wall. Pain seared down my limb and numbness curled up my neck.

Sean grabbed me. "Are you okay, Dad? Dad?"

I raised my hand and felt a lump on the back of my head. That oddly didn't hurt as much as my limb. "Uh-huh."

Bret descended the ladder and immediately asked, "Where's Malcom?"

"Didn't make it," I said.

Grace immediately questioned, "Why didn't you pull him up?"

Not wanting to alarm my son of a polar bear in the vicinity, I said, "He was dragged away with the current. No way I could have reached him."

Grace covered her eyes with her hands and began rocking back and forth. Balancing himself, Bret stood over my body. "This is the S.S. Alaska. I discovered this sunken sub while looking for Al. It's solid. There was a hole in the lowest end where it sank. Someone sealed the section and they'll probably be back in the spring to retrieve the sub once the ice thaws."
I took in a deep breath; my head was pounding. Unfocused, my eyes suddenly blurred on Bret's face. I leaned heavily against the wall as darkness overwhelmed me.

Chapter 15

I woke to a loud explosive noise. My eyes flew open to find the hatch
being ripped off and three massive creatures leaping down beside the
ladder. Their fangs were dripping blood. Their claws were shooting
out from their fingertips like giant cats.
Bret grabbed one of my legs. Grace and Sean snatched the other and
pulled me out of the next cabin. The beasts ran after us.
Bret slammed doors. The beasts crashed through as we came into a
room where we had no way out.
"There's no door! We're trapped," Grace said.
The six animals began spreading out and encircling us, pressuring
us back against the wall.
"Leave us alone!" Grace said.
One creature came closer and towered over me, his red eyes piercing
down. I hadn't seen anything so frightening before or so beautiful. In
the center of the red pupil was a shade of purple lining the outside. It
got bigger and smaller, depending on the way the creature cocked his
head. Underneath its furry nose, I could easily see long incisors. They
appeared like vampire's teeth. I couldn't tear my eyes away, staring
straight at hell's weapon.
Slowly, the beast raised a set of sharp claws and placed them on my
shoulder, imbedding them deeply into my flesh.
I cried out.
Bret tried to raise the giant nails but to no avail. The creature pushed
him away as if to say, "nice try."

"Do you understand me?" I asked.

"Ra Madahna Dey." It spoke in the exact tone as I had just used. "Ra Ra doh ma…ka ni."

"My name is Adam," I said. "I know we must look strange to you. Believe us, you appear different to us, but that doesn't mean we have to be enemies."

The creature's hair on the top of his head stood up and shook. "What does that mean?" Grace asked.

"When creatures show off it's a sign of dominance." I lowered my eyes. "Do what I do, lower your head to show him your respect."

Quickly Grace lowered her face and Bret dropped to his knees, paying tribute to these white demons. A beast snatched Grace, pulling her into his arms.

"Let me go!" she demanded.

I tried to rise but claws dug deeper into my shoulder, then came another hand around my neck. It didn't choke me but instead kept me down.

"Help!" Grace cried out.

I pulled at the furry arms around me, but before I could break free, Grace's attacker bit her neck with long incisors. Her eyes rolled back into her head and her lifeless body was thrown to the floor.

With blood staining his white face, the creature then snatched Bret, ripped off his head in one quick swoop, and kicked down his body. The others dove in and began consuming Bret and Grace's corpses on the floor.

I gave my son a push. "Run to the ladder! Now!"

"I won't leave you!"

I felt sharp pains in my chest. My eyes lowered and saw that claws were now digging deeply into my chest. "Run!"

"Dad! Dad!"

My body shook. My eyes flashed open and found my son above me. "Dad, you hit your head real bad. Dad, can you hear me?"

I sat up. Bret and Grace were watching from a distance. I glanced around the room, no corpses. Everyone was alive! My heart thumped as I witnessed worried expressions gazing back. Their deaths had been just a dream.

Chapter 16

"Does your head hurt, Adam?" Grace asked.
Feeling dizzy, I slowly stood. "How long was I out for?"
"A few minutes," she replied.
"Where did my flashlight go?" I asked.
She grabbed a flashlight from her belt and tossed it to me.
"We should have a look around the rest of the sub." I turned on the
light. "We need to find supplies."
The group of us began moving through the hallway. The back was
dark. The flashlight inched across the metal walls and in the rooms.
Searching up and down overturned desks and broken chairs, we
pressed on. I could see the breath coming from my mouth and guessed
this part of the sub was underwater. The light skipped across the
sidewall where I discovered a porthole. A seal was on the other side
squashing his nose against the glass.
"Dad, are you sure you're okay?"
"Yes." I removed my jacket and placed it over my son's shoulders.
"Are you cold?"
 "But you'll freeze," Sean said.
"I'm all right," I replied.
We moved deeper into the sub. There were photos in the hall of
many men in navy uniform and one half of a torn picture of a young
girl with golden curly hair.
"Why do you think the crew all abandoned ship?" Grace asked.

"When the wet hull went into the glacier, it took in water which froze the sub in place," Bret said.

We traveled further down the hall until we came upon two hatches, one on the right side and another to our left. I touched the right door.

It felt like touching ice so I pulled my hand away. "This must have water behind it." I then tried the other hatch. It was cold but not painfully so.

I handed the flashlight to my son. "Keep it on the door." I grabbed the hatch wheel.

"What if there's water?" Grace asked me.

"If it starts seeping in, I'll retighten the lock."

"Are you sure about this?" Bret asked.

"They could have blankets and food on the other side."

Bret nodded in agreement and grabbed the wheel too. "On three," he said.

"One, two, three!" We began turning the wheel.

Sean bent down to see if any water was spilling out; there were none.

"All clear." The hatch cracked open. Sean praised. "No water."

I slowly swung the door as the flashlight quickly went to find what was in the room. Blood had dropped from the ceiling and down the walls. There were no dead bodies, only a Teddy Bear with the words "I love Dad" written across its chest, sitting in the corner.

Opening the closest dresser drawer, hoping to find blankets or extra clothing, I was surprised inside was dripping blood. "Where did this come from?"

"Here, Dad." Sean tossed the flashlight back to me.

With the light, I moved around the dresser searching for the source of the blood. Behind it was a door. I quickly discovered an empty bathroom. There was a Captain's hat in the sink. Everything reflected silver except for red-stained hand marks across the back of the shower.

Wedged between two metal posts, the shower door blocked a hole in the sub. In the deep crystal water, a giant white furry mass swam towards the sub with back legs swimming like a mermaid. The fish began jumping away in every direction.

Terror gripped every inch of my body.

With a sudden burst of speed, the creature smacked against the glass. The white furry massive creature shoved the door aside. Water burst inside. Like lightning, we fled. The white beast was coming inside. Grace ran through the hatch. I grabbed the sub door. Bret slammed it and we began to turn the wheel to keep the water and beast out.

The creature pushed hard, making large indentations in the door. I jumped back, wondering if the door was going to break, but then only the water swooshing could be heard.

The flashlight flickered. Blackness came, followed by silence.

Chapter 17

"Dad, what should we do now?"

"Now what?" Bret asked me.

"We need to stay calm."

As I hit the flashlight against my leg, it flickered on and I began leading them back toward the main compartment. Grace stopped under the ladder; her eyes glanced upward.

I realized that the creatures had stopped their break in attempts and wondered for how long? Were they plotting something? Had they forgotten we'd become their prize dinner?

My eyes scanned the room. Over the overturned desks and chairs I caught a black box attached to the wall. I went and opened it. Inside sat a small bottle of scotch. "What do you think, Grace? Should we polish this?"

"I've got a little more on my mind than getting drunk again with you, Adam."

"Dad, please. Don't!"

Bret snatched the bottle out of my hand. "Isn't that what destroyed your marriage?"

"What the hell is that supposed to mean?" I replied.

"We all know." Bret gulped down a few sips.

"It's not your business."

"It is when ours depend on you keeping your head on straight!" Bret snipped. "If there's any time to quit it should be now."

"At least I never did what you did."

"That was low." Bret took another sip. "Now it's my fault that you became a drunk. She came over to my apartment to talk about how rotten of a husband you'd become. She fell asleep on the sofa. I carried her to bed, closed the door, and slept on the couch. You kicked her out of the house, filed divorce papers, and for what? This?"
Grabbing Bret by the shirt, I shoved him against the wall as tears welled. "You Bastard!"
"I never slept with her, Adam," Bret said.
"You did with half the crew in Georgia, LA, Atlanta; must I go on!"
Bret straightened his shirt back down over his tight abs.
"But not her."
I snatched the bottle from him. The pain of losing Mary was welling up inside me all over again. It was hard enough to look at him and remember our past. "You're lying."
"You walked in on her fully dressed underneath the covers. You and that bull head of yours never even asked what happened."
"I went home and she never returned."
"Would you want to come home to you?" Bret raised his hands. "At least you've still got the bottle to keep you company."
"You don't know how hard it was. I didn't want her to see me falling apart."
"You had a great wife, a top-notch kid, and you threw it away and blamed her. You're the one who should be dead now!"
"Enough!" Grace yelled. "Adam, Bret's right. You need to keep a clear head."
For a moment, I looked at the scotch in the bottle, wanting it more than ever. Slowly, Grace took it out of my hands.
Sean wrapped his arms around me, making it clear how happy I had just made my son.
Bret rolled his eyes and went to the door. He put his ear against it to listen. Then he backed away and sat down on the floor. "I don't like this. They're quiet."

"Maybe that big mouth of yours scared em' off," Grace said, consuming the rest of the scotch herself.

Chapter 18

Huddled together, we slept through the night. I at least attempted to.
Every creaking sound made me shift, along with Bret's words which
haunted my dreams.
The moment Bret woke, I had to admit, "You were right. I blamed
Mary when it was my drinking that ruined everything. My wife is
gone and there's nothing I can do. She died, hating me."
Bret said, "I didn't mean it to come out so coldly."
Lying next to me, Sean suddenly jumped up. One furry beast was
staring in the porthole, a clawed paw leaning against the glass.
"Will it break?" Grace sat up.
Bret grabbed the camera and began taping the creature in the window.
"Adam, shine the light so I can get a good take."
The rays moved to the beveled glass window to scare it off. The
beast had this sad look in his eyes. I came closer and peered into the
shimmering red pupils.
Bret said, "This is picking up the scale, how big its head is in
comparison to yours."
"What's wrong?" I spoke to the white furry mass. "We're not going
to be your dinner, after all?"
Suddenly a strange buzzing noise came from above, growing louder.
I knew immediately and a thrill seared through my veins. "Plane!"
"We can't get to the station!" Grace gasped.
As I peered back at the porthole, the creature was no longer there.
"Like hell we'll miss it!" I hurried up the ladder and began opening
the door's hatch.

"Wait!" Bret warned.

"It's our only chance. They'll think we're among the dead." With
the last turn, I peered out and found that the creatures weren't there.
The coast was clear. "Let's go. Don't look back!"

"Are any still up there?" Sean asked.

"Gone." I jumped out and lowered my hand to help Grace up.
Within a few seconds we were in the cold air, searching for the
creatures with the roar of the airplane growing louder.

"The plane noises scared them off." Bret put the camera inside his
jacket.

The four of us ran for Polar II in the distance. The plane was heading
straight toward the building.

Wham!

From below the snow a white furry hand grabbed my leg, tripping
me. "Dad!"

"Go!" I yelled.

The giant beast jumped from the snow and rushed after Sean and
Grace. With fur flying, more creatures began popping out of the snow
around me, five of them. Like wet dogs, they rose, shaking off the ice.
The plane landed. My heart pounded as one creature might catch
up to them before it rolled to a full stop. In retrospect, I realized we
should have waited until the plane landed. It wouldn't be long until the
largest beast would catch up to Sean and Grace.

Feeling claws on my legs, I snatched the flare gun from my jacket.
I whipped around and faced the five creatures standing around my
body. Hearing Sean's screams, I raised the flare gun to explode into
the chest of the center creature.

Suddenly, all the beasts raised their hands. One stepped back, the
others followed his lead, as if saying, "Don't shoot."

I couldn't believe it. "You all know what a gun is?"

The center creature reached up to his head and yanked off the fur. Before me stood Saul Cannon, leader of Polar II, one furry white mask in his clawed hand.

"Saul?"

"Don't shoot, Adam! It's me."

The beasts beside him pulled off their masks. A blonde woman with big blue eyes appeared. The breath left my body. I gasped out a sigh of anger mixed with relief. Never had I been so stunned, yet so thrilled.

"Mary?"

"Ken!" Saul called.

Chapter 19

Chasing Bret, Grace, and Sean to the plane, the creature immediately halted and returned to stand next to Adam's body. "Hi, Adam." Removing his headdress, a man revealed salt and pepper hair and a long beard.

It wasn't long before Bret, Grace, and Sean circled around and hurried over to the group.

"Ken Peters?" Grace gasped.

Sean ran for his mother. "Mom, you're okay!"

"Why did you bring him?" Mary glared at Adam.

"Oh, no, you aren't going to blame this on me. I wanted our son to have an adventure. I didn't think his mother was going to try and scare the living daylights out of us."

Grace stepped forward and slapped the older man's face. "Is this some kind of joke?"

I rose and grabbed Bret's camera. He hit eject. Out popped the video tape. "Is this why, Saul?"

Saul slowly nodded yes. "And it was even worth pouring skunk and monkey urine all over me for. You noticed that smell, didn't you?"

"They scared us on purpose." Sean stepped back to stand beside his father.

"Ken, I told him to because I wanted to tell you everything in the cave of what was happening. Your father rushed in and saved you before I could explain," Mary said.

"How could you do this? I thought you were dead, Mom!"

Out of the three remaining masked creatures, two removed their cover. Out popped dreadlocks from the tallest man; the other showed a familiar dark face.

"Well, if it isn't Malcom still alive, and his brother Jason Carson." Grace gasped. I shoved the flare gun back into my jacket. "Was your death even staged, Malcom? How'd you pull that one off, all that blood and guts movie magic? Was the bear real?"

"We brought in Maggie from the zoo. Our biggest fear was that you would recognize the polar bear from your visits so we made her gain some weight and put fake blood on her fur," Malcom said.

"Whatever it takes to make the mighty dollar, right?"

"The whole idea was mine," Bret admitted.

I glared. "So you were in on this?"

"Listen, you know as well as I do how much Planet X makes off of our documentaries," Bret said. "We already came out and made Jack's crap about polar bears. We're going to sell the fake Bigfoot movie to the highest bidder on the underground market."

"So Grace and I were sent here as stooges in your screenplay?"

"We needed to capture real fear." Bret shrugged. "We didn't know you were bringing Sean. We almost backed out when we saw him."

"Almost!" Grace shouted. "He's just a kid. This was low, Bret, even for you. So who's this last one, Mike?" she asked the only remaining creature still wearing a mask.

The creature lowered its head, nodding yes. "We'll all be millionaires," Bret promised.

"What about my son?" I asked Mary. "Was scaring him worth it?" Sean couldn't look at any of them.

"It's a good lesson for any kid to learn," Bret said. "The only real monster in this life is greed."

"I only played a part because I needed money for a divorce lawyer. Then I started thinking, if you didn't take a drink through all this, than maybe, maybe you were really serious when you said you'd stop," Mary said.

"Dad may have been a drunk," Sean yelled, "but at least he's not a liar, Mom!"

Her eyes filled with tears. "You didn't take a drink, did you, Adam? We left bottles in the Snowcat and on the sub. You didn't even take a sip."

"I told you I was going on the wagon."

Her hand rose to her eyes and she wiped away tears. "I never slept with Bret, you know?"

Adam nodded. "You left because of my drinking."

"I don't even want a divorce. I just wanted our family back the way it was."

"You screwed up this reunion." I lowered the videotape to my side.

"I wanted the man I married back," Mary admitted. "And I certainly didn't think you would bring Sean here. You were supposed to take him to Aunt Lucy's, remember?"

"Well, excuse me for wanting to bring our son to visit his mother. I didn't realize she had this freaky morbid side who wanted to scare the crap out of him!"

"Well, at least we know you stopped drinking. If you didn't during this, you probably won't ever again," Bret said.

"Don't even..." Adam pointed. "That doesn't change that the first

thing I'm doing on the airplane is to call Jack and tell him what's going on!"

Saul snatched the film out of my hands and quickly handed it to the only masked creature. "Mike, put this in the safe."

The creature rushed away.

Saul poked Adam's chest. "You aren't going to spoil this for me. We'll give you all a fair cut of the money, even for the kid."

"Like hell I'll be any part of this scam!" I shoved him back.

Grace moved between us, quickly interrupting. "How much?"

Chapter 20

A hint of sparkle reflected in Saul's brilliant emerald eyes. The five o'clock shadow around his bluish lips swayed ever so slightly. "Millions, Baby," was how he put it.

Grace breathed deeply as if shocked by the financial goal. "I'm willing to forget about authenticity."

"Think about it, Adam." Mary held her hands up. "You can finally get that Garnet Hummer."

"Lowering yourself to bribery, Mary?"

"What about Sean?" she asked, treating me rather offensively. "We can buy him that RX2987 bike."

"I'd give that bike away if I could have my family back the way it was before Dad started drinking and you started hanging out with Bret," Sean said.

I closed my eyes. The pain of those words seared through me like a knife. My son always wanted to impress his friends with that fancy bike. It was a symbol of wealth and popularity. Sean didn't care about that as much as my stopping drinking. Have I really been this bad? I wondered. Look what I've done to an innocent boy and a woman that used to go to church every Sunday.

"Dad," Sean asked, "what do you want?"

"AA. The hell ends."

Sean hugged me. He hadn't embraced me so tightly since he was baby clutching on my arm with tiny fingers. This was one of those hugs only a father can appreciate. He was my kid and he truly loved me.

Looking up to my wife, I softly muttered, "I've hurt you both and I see
what my drinking has done. I'm sorry. I couldn't even blame you
if you had slept with Bret."

"We didn't," Bret said, "unfortunately."

"No, you didn't." I grinned, pleased. "But you did have enough time to
turn my wife into someone willing to take money for a non-existent
species. Perhaps I drove her to the edge, but you pushed her over."

Mary shrugged her small shoulders. The scorn in her voice turned
to pleading. "This isn't anyone's fault. We can all work together and
make a fortune here."

"My satisfaction comes from transporting animals where they won't be
hunted by greedy poachers. You want a payout for lying to the public? I
don't believe that is a good way to make a living. There's no
justification."

In a flash, Bret reached in my jacket, grabbed the orange flare gun,
and pointed it directly at my chest. It happened in an instant with no
time to react. Had I the chance, I surely would have throttled him with
the gun myself.

"Then I guess you'll have to die," Bret exploded, tightening his grip
on the weapon.

"Drop it!" Mary begged.

"You'll forgive me after you get the money, Mary." With a knowing
gleam in his eyes, he grinned like a crocodile.

"Just leave Adam on this island. The polar bears will get him soon
enough," Saul suggested.

"Then I'll return to the states and tell the press that film is nothing
but a fake," Adam said.

Bret laughed half-heartedly. "Like anyone would believe a drunk.
Mary, I'm going to ask. You know how I feel about you. Come with
me and be filthy rich. Stay here and die. What is your choice?"

Mary didn't answer. She shook her head no, but her blue gems flashed
yes. She paced a few steps then looked over at me as if I would

speak for her. Those days were over. This was her decision, Bret or me, so I shut my mouth, waiting for the reply to come.

"I don't know about her." Grace's expression turned from one of worry to confidence. "But I'm with you, Bret, as long as you don't kill Adam."

"And you won't label the film a fake?" Bret asked her.

"I'll take the money."

Mary bit her upper lip and made her choice. "Okay. I'll go, Bret, but nothing happens to my husband. Just leave him and I'll fly back in a few weeks after we sell the tape. There's food in Polar II and Adam can handle the elements and wild life until then."

I had to turn away. She had once been such an angel with a heart of gold, but now I hardly recognized her. "What happened to my sweet wife?"

"I have to make sure I can afford to live if you fail and start drinking again so our son can go to college and have some kind of a future instead of picking his drunken daddy off the floor!"

I felt the gun press again into my chest. It wasn't a pleasant feeling knowing Bret not only hated me but also wanted me dead if I attempted to stop them. Chills ran down my spine, but it wasn't fear or the cold, only rage. The feeling, I'm sure, was mutual.

"Start walking," Bret said in a disconcerting tone.

Sean grasped my arm. He raised his spiked haired head, tightened his gaze, and said with such conviction, "I'm staying with my Dad."

"No, you're not!" Mary came at him. He spit at her with an intolerant mouth.

She stopped in her tracks, shocked he would do such a thing. Her eyes narrowed with mother's revenge pondering over options of disciplining. Then her expression softened almost as if she concluded Sean had the right to be angry. Slowly, she moved to face him.

"You can't force me, Mom. I'll rat you out! I'll tell everyone at school, anyone who will listen."

"The kid stays," Bret decreed.

"Your father can survive." Mary snatched the edge of Sean's jacket, but he pushed her hand away. "Please, son, you must come with me!"

"You can stay too, Mary, but then you can't return for them after we've sold the film." Bret's attention returned to Sean and me. "Of course if some polar bear chews up your two bodies in the meantime, that might be good for our ratings." The flare gun then directed at Mary's torso as Bret's reptilian smile returned.

"Coming, Dear?"

Chapter 21

Mike returned with an announcement, white fur no longer covering his head and the videotape missing from his hand. At this distance, I couldn't make out Mike's large-boned features but I recognized his enormous seven-foot height. We met briefly at a Fourth of July party Planet X held where he bragged about how many hundreds of pounds he could lift body building. Born in Great Britain, Mike talked slightly with an accent, loud, bossy and arrogant.

"The plane's arrived! Let's get bloody rich!" Mike yelled. Oh, yeah, that's him, I thought.

"Mary, board the plane," Bret demanded. "Malcom, do what's necessary while Saul and I take care of business."

Suddenly Bret grabbed my arm and Saul nudged Sean forward. With the light of a flashlight, through the driven snow we traipsed toward the mountain where Sean had been previously kept. The cave would provide warmth and shelter. The food at Polar I should nourish us until Mary returned. A wave of relief raced down my spine, as I realized we might make it out of this mess alive.

Even ticked off, I wanted to see Mary once more before we disappeared over the bank. I glanced back and saw her watching. Mary's long blonde hair whipped in the cold wind and her eyebrows were half way to her forehead with worry. I had first touched that hair by accident, I recalled, dancing in Rio in a small cottage by a river as a guitarist played Spanish music on an acoustic. I wasn't into the salsa, but when I saw Mary swaying her hips in the center of the floor, I had to get closer. After the next song, I wormed beside Mary and her partner. She twisted and twirled as my hand shot up. A lock of her blonde hair caught between my fingers. I relished the soft touch of the strand as Mary yelped out in pain. That moment, our eyes locked. I saw her thin nose and big luscious pink lips so close. While trapping and moving wildlife in South America, I didn't expect to meet an American, especially one that appeared like the girl next door, yet every part of her was different. That very second, I gave this beauty my heart.

Over the years, her face slightly aged, her hips grew a little wider, but none of that mattered. To me she was every bit as sensational as on that dance floor, even her personality was as spicy as the hot Latin music. Enjoying outdoors, fishing, and sports, even in front of the cameras, she lit up like a tamale. She was more than what I deserved in a wife. There were many happy years before I started drinking.

With the air temperature dropping and the sun vanishing from the sky, the plane lights and the flashlight lit up the canyon as we traveled to the mountain's edge.

"You're not going to hang me upside down again?" Sean asked Saul.

"No," Saul said.

I gazed to the cave's high entrance. We'd be safe enough, from everything but what could climb like the leopard. Arctic animals are white not to be seen by the naked eye, allowing prey to become omnipotent and the hunter approach undetected. The snow leopard is no different. It's a stunning silvery white and one of the most elusive creatures in the world. It hunts, lives, and dies alone. With a feeding territory ranging several miles, it is one of the least recorded animals. Not much is known, but this mighty cat remains feared. Descendant of the saber tooth tiger, its enormous paws contain razor claws and a mouth full of sharp teeth only a vampire could appreciate.

With the flare gun pointed at our backs, Sean and I climbed the boulders. Saul and Bret followed. Bret helped Sean with a boost up the third most treacherous rock.

"You'll be fine," Bret said, sarcastically. "Just remember not to cut yourself." Sean looked at me, fear written across his face.

"We'll make it through," I reassured Sean, quickly, trying not to think of the deadly white feline.

From this height, I could make out the front of the plane with the letters PLANET X coming together in a point. Jack had sent the company jet instead of the cargo. A group, the size of ants at this distance, headed toward the plane, among them one with long blonde hair.

She boarded first, then two individuals headed back down the stairs and inside Polar I. They reentered the plane, clutching a large brown trunk. It didn't take me long to figure out there was only one thing in Polar I worth taking. "The brothers are taking our food."

Saul glanced in the direction of the plane. "Well, what do you know."

"No!" Sean gasped.

They brought us further inside the cave, taking us into the first large opening. Bret demanded we sit. As we maneuvered onto the cold ice, Saul extracted some rope from under his coat and started tying Sean's and my hands together, back-to-back.

After finishing, Bret paced, gazing over his tying handy work. Then from a pant pocket, he extended a switch blade knife, flipping it open. Taking a step, he shined the silver in front of Sean's face with his blue eyes gleaming like the devil. I was fearful of what he might do. "Leave my boy alone!" I demanded, protectively.

"What Mary doesn't know can't hurt her." Bret took a step away from Sean and quickly sliced my arm. The blade slashed from my shoulder to my elbow. The deep cut made me wince in pain, but Bret didn't even have to explain why this sudden violent action was necessary. Blood attracts vicious scavengers. With the injury scent lurking in the air, there wouldn't be enough of us left by dawn. "You're leaving us to die by the leopard," I said, "and you're taking both Mary and the money."

"I always have a backup plan." Bret gave another crocodile grin. "There won't be anything for Mary to return to."

Our assailants began retreating, taking our only source of light, the flashlight. Feeling the blood pouring down my arm, I begged for my son's life. "Don't leave Sean, Bret. Take him. He won't say a thing."

"If he discredits the film it wouldn't be worth anything, now would it?"

"Bret, please, he's Mary's son too."

"That he is."

"Then spare his life for her," I begged.

"She'll have me to lean on during our grief," he said. "I'm sure she'll need lots of comforting losing both her husband and son all at once."

Through the darkness, Bret whirled the flashlight back around and shined it on Sean's face. "No hard feelings, Kid. You're about to meet the real monsters of the ice your father warned you about. Just be thankful you'll never grow up to be a greedy son-of-a-bitch like me." With the light gone, the cave darkened. All I could hear was the sudden cry of my son tied behind me.

Chapter 22

There came a temporary, deceptive peace until the hairs on the back of my arms stood up. Listening to my son's cries, I knew my sudden despair wasn't from his being so upset.

Another rustle came from the cave's entrance. Trying to see through the dark, I saw shadows move. I shivered from more than the cold, hearing the crunch of feet moving methodically in.

"Son, are you moving?" I asked him.

"Dad, what's that noise?"

Swish! Swish! Swish!

"Who's there?" I asked the darkness.

Inches from my face, red eyes suddenly appeared. Facing the devil himself, my body shot back. Then as quickly as they shined, those shimmering eyes vanished.

"You see anything?" Sean asked. "What's the matter?"

Another shuffling across the floor negotiated steps of my unwelcome discovery. Consciousness slowly and fuzzily returned; I decided I had to fight whatever that was with my hands tied behind my back.

Swish! Swish! Swish!

"Dad?"

"Don't be alarmed," I explained. "There's an animal in the cave, maybe a fox or something."

"A big animal?"

The size of those crimson gems, which were in close range to the Bigfoot creatures, I remembered seeing through the pane of glass. One difference, these round pupils appeared octagon. How bazaar! What in these parts could have eyes like that? A bear's eyes were nothing similar. "I don't know."

Swish! Swish! Swish! A spark lit up the cave.

Sean let out a cry of horror.

I discovered the impossible. In the center of the cave above a pile of logs an enormous white furred creature held a log with burning flames at one tip. In an instant, he dropped the lit branch into the pile. Bigfoot, Yeti, the Abominable Snowman, whatever you call it doesn't give it justice; large hands, massive feet, and the smell grew quick and hideously, more potent than a skunk's spray. Horrid stench filled the cave, making my eyes water.

Beside his tree trunk legs, a snow leopard sat. Around the thick cat's neck was a leash made of rope. This incredible panther-sized feline, just slightly smaller than India's striped tiger, was stealth, heavy, and silver like snow. Long whiskers twitched as a hiss escaped through giant teeth. How rare it was to even catch a glimpse of such a magnificent mammal! In another time and place, it would have thrilled me to my very core.

Wondering how any of the crew trapped the world's most elusive cat and trained it to walk by rope, I quickly questioned, "When did the zoo capture a snow leopard?"

The logs enflamed and the cave brightened and warmed as my son and I waited for a response. For quite some time, the beast sat down on a boulder, avoiding us.

"Who are you?" I looked him over, noticing the enormous build of this creature. Only Mike had such an impressive frame with huge biceps that he had gotten from years of professional bodybuilding. "Mike?"

"Dad, look." Sean had his face turned toward the entrance of the cave.

I pivoted from the monster and saw a pile of small zebra colored fish. I couldn't smell anything but the beast, so I assumed they were frozen. "Great, sushi tonight."

Suddenly the creature rose and paced. I didn't take my eyes off him, staring at the costume trying to figure out which nemesis this was and where the zipper sat underneath the long hair. Guessing by the size this beast must be seven-foot Mike who appeared taller since we were seated, I determined.

"Mike, is that you under there?"

The creature grabbed a large stone near the fish and raised it above his head. "Dad," Sean warned. "Look out!"

Thinking the beast was going to throw it and strike either one of us dead, I begged, "I'll go along with the film story all right; just don't hurt my son. We did see Bigfoot in the snow! We did! Yeti tons of them. The biggest primates I've ever seen."

With a mighty heave came the rock.

I cried out just as the rock shot out and split the rope between our hands. I took a deep breath as the creature bent over and twirled the rope.

"You're freeing us," I spoke, surprisingly. The creature moved to the front of the cave. "Hurry, son," I demanded.

"I'm trying."

He went to the ropes in the middle of my legs, tossed down the rock. With the first strike the rope cut in half and I jumped to my feet.

"You're good, Dad!"

Suddenly with a mighty roar, the creature fled into the darkness of the night with the sleek leopard pouncing by his side.

"Wait!" I jumped up and ran after the creature and its pet, demanding answers. Who came back to bring us food and fire? I hurried to the front of the cave but the two were no longer inside.

"Be careful, Dad," warned Sean. "We don't know what that is."

Needing light to travel further, I ran back, grabbed a log enflamed on one end, and hurried to the cave's entrance. Through the mist I saw a white furry mass jump thirty feet down the mountain of ice and land on its feet with the cat cradled in its arms. Slowly, he turned back, lowering the cat to the snow. Its red eyes were piercing.

"Thank you!" I yelled.
The beast and its pet raced from the range of the light. Still wondering who had just saved our lives, I returned to my son.
In his hand was a black and white striped fish with a chunk missing out of the middle. "It isn't that bad, really."

One Week Later...

Chapter 23

In the darkness of night, red and yellow blinking lights lowered onto the plains below.

"Is that a plane landing?" Sean questioned.

With the heavy snow, and the temperature dropping, I reassured him. "Looks that way, but we'll have to wait until morning. It's too dangerous to traverse the mountain until dawn."

Sean seated himself in front of the fire. "Do you think Mom came back like she promised?"

"I don't know. I'm not very happy with her at the moment," I admitted.

"Me either," he grumbled. "I'm not even sure I want to see her again."

Sitting by the fire, I patted him softly across the shoulder. "She's still your mother and although we don't agree with her decisions, she thinks she's doing what's best."

"Sounds like a cop-out."

"She loves you and deep down, me too. We just have to remember what I put her through and that's why she took drastic measures."

"You've stopped drinking!"

"Your mother isn't convinced. It will just take time. Right now, we have more pressing matters," I glanced out into the darkness to the flickering lights, "like if that's friend or foe."

Sean huffed. "I've been thinking about that big monster who untied us. He was freakier."

Remembering the octagon shape of the pupils, I smiled, "He wore different contacts, that's all. Whoever that was didn't want to be recognized; that's why he never removed his mask. By the height, I'm guessing, it was Mike."

"Don't you believe in the Yeti, Dad?" he asked, curiously. "Out here on this island, don't you think it's possible for a creature to survive and not be found?"

"I won't be tricked again."

Sean rose from the fire and went to the wall. "What about this, Dad?"

To the back of the cave, I traveled to the enormous sketch for a closer look. The lines were crooked and not well defined, the meaning significant. A beast locked in a cage with a man holding a spear. I'd first seen it when I came to rescue Sean from his kidnappers.

I touched the black drawing right above the beast's hairline. Like chalk, it smudged by my quick touch. Unreadable scribbled letters scrolled above. Across the cave ceiling was a different sketch of a plane crashing.

"Dad, these drawings must stand for something."

"It's another attempt to scare us," I determined.

Hearing a thud behind us, I pivoted. Smoke blackened the fire.

Inside the flames, an object burned black and square. I hurried over and discovered a videotape with "Yeti" written on top.

Frantically, I turned around. Whoever laid the videotape had vanished.

Encircling the fire were footprints, large ones, three times the size of mine. "Dad, is that Bret's tape?"

"It's the million-dollar false proof of the Bigfoot's existence," I said, surprised.

"That's weird." Sean took in a deep breath. "Why would Bret come back and burn the tape that could make him so much money, Dad?"

I lowered the log to make it burn faster. "I don't know, but we'll probably find out soon." Hoping that it was Mary on that plane that landed and not Bret, I said, "I pray your mother is still on our side and came to give us the answers."

Chapter 24

Flipping back the hood on her coat, Mary entered the cave. Her hands and body were shivering. As pale as a ghost she made her way to sit by the fire. Shocked and with mixed emotions, I wondered if I should trust her.

Sean took off his coat and laid it across her shoulders, "This will help until the fire warms you, Mom."

Mary gave it back. "We have more to worry about. When we got

to the states, Mike said he didn't have the tape. We all watched you hand it to him; now he's denying it. They've flown back, thinking you made a switch. We have to find a way off this island before morning." Her eyes drew into the fire where the last of the video, a corner was burning.

"The tape's gone, Mom," Sean admitted.

She was still shaking. "Are you any warmer?" I asked.

She smiled. "I'll be okay."

I couldn't stop myself from returning the gesture. "You don't even look upset that the video is destroyed."

"You and Sean mean more to me than anything. I would have stayed before if I was sure they'd come back."

Looking deeply into her blue eyes, I could tell she meant it. I leaned in to kiss her cold lips. Before I could fully enjoy the connection, I heard the pounding of footsteps. Slowly, I pivoted from her, with an overwhelming rush of doom running down my spine.

"I love you, Adam. I wouldn't have gotten so upset about what you

were doing to yourself if I didn't. Please, don't turn away now."

Shaking off snow, Bret and Saul stomped in, interrupting. Seven foot tall, Mike towered behind them. "Isn't this precious? I knew she'd lead us straight back here in the dark. Where the hell is our tape, Adam?"

I pointed to the towering man with the long goatee. "You know who I handed it to."

Mike shot back, "That's a lie!"

"When you were threatening, Bret, I clearly handed Mike the tape. I had no choice!" I reminded.

"It wasn't me!" Mike claimed.

"Where the hell else were you, McDonald's?" Bret snapped. "So you're sticking to what he says? You have no idea where the tape is either? Maybe you both are in this together!"

Inside the flames, I saw the last of the tape turning to ash. Was Mike telling the truth? I had handed the tape to the largest man wearing a mask or was he double- crossing everyone? Was that even the right tape?

"So, what's the real story?" Bret asked me.

"You saw," I reminded him.

"We scanned the video and what's there is nothing but polar bears."

"Isn't that what you came here to film?" I asked, finding it highly ironic. "I'm sure Jack appreciated getting what he paid for."

Bret suddenly lashed out. "I should beat the hell out of you and your kid until one of you tells me where my tape is!"

I caught his fist in the palm of my hand.

"That's my husband and my son you're threatening!" Mary gasped.

Instantly Bret pushed me, knocking me to the ground. He leaped on top of me. I avoided punches by shoving Bret back. He grabbed my wrist, snapping off my watch. Now pissed, when he lunged again, I quickly helicopter kicked him across the jaw. His body hit the ice with a thud.

"You're acting like a beast," I said.

"Oh, I've just begun." Bret sat up, rubbing his cheek.

"This is over. We're getting on that plane and going home or I'll kick your ass one very piece of this berg!" I promised.

Mary kneeled down to Bret's side, checking out his lip bleeding down his chin. "He's right, Bret, let this go."

Over Mike's shoulder I could see the sun gleaming in the east. Soon, I hoped to be away from this ice land and live in Florida overlooking the warm blue ocean.

"We'd have to bring more suits and come up with an excuse for Planet X to film here again. You know as well as I, Adam will tell Jack then. The only way we could pull this off is to kill him, Mary and Sean. If you even tried, I would tell the police myself," Saul said.

Bret rushed at me, but Saul immediately punched him in the face, finishing the job I started.

Suddenly Grace entered. "So who's at fault?" she asked.

Mike sighed. "Let's forget we were ever here."

"Let's," Saul said in agreement.

"When the tape vanished so did the lies. This island doesn't even exist," I concluded.

Grace and Saul descended the mountain first. Mike tossed Bret over one massive shoulder and leaped down. When Sean and Mary trailed to the edge, I realized my watch was still on the ice inside. The time piece Mary gave me on our first wedding anniversary.

"I'll be right back." I went to retrieve my watch. "We'll wait at the bottom of the mountain," Mary said.

When I reentered the ice cave's main room, a creature was sitting next to the fire. My mouth widened to cry out, but I shut it instead, thinking twice.

Slowly, I leaned down, picked up my leather band. "You are what you are, aren't you?"

"What he is," came a strange deep voice beside me, "is more than you."

My eyes shifted to a thick leg covered in long white fur. Staying motionless, my heart pounded as I wondered what to do.

Chapter 25

The small yeti's red eyes were fragmented with pigments of gold, truly amazing spectacles. Around the pupils, there were no lines indicating contacts.

The young beast raised his head as if curious about me too. With passionate appreciation my heart pounded. I raised a shaky hand to the

small furry head and gently patted.

"Aaagh," the larger creature grunted.

Wondering if my touch wasn't approved, I bravely turned over the young one's hand, comparing it with my own. It had five fingers but different from a human's. The bottoms were black and tough like those of an ape. I moved the white furred hand to my cheek and relished its softness. Slowly, claws retracted from the tips. Quickly, I decided it was better to release my grip.

The larger beast let out a yelp.

The hair on the back of my arms stood. He moved closer, standing a good seven feet above me. The smell had a rank odor matching the one who untied us. I stood and thought it best to back away from the child in case the parent thought its nails came out in fear.

The large creature didn't take his eyes off of us, protectively. I surmised its high intelligence. Was this the one who freed us? Did it even put the tape in the fire?

The beast slammed its hand on the wall right above the drawing of a plane leaving with the Yeti cheering in approval. It raised its arms in a similar fashion and again pounded against the rock.

I got the unvocal message. It was telling me, in no uncertain terms, to leave.

To my right a giant boulder of ice rolled. Behind it, out came another, a heavier beast with large furry breasts. The young one ran. The female swept it up and it gripped onto her back, piggyback style.

Were there others on the other side, a whole community, of males, females, and more offspring?

I trembled as a tear ran down my cheek, finding myself half in shock, half in fear. Books written previously labeled Yeti as monsters, but not I. That's not how I see them. They are intelligent, beautiful, elusive, and a creature too independent to ever survive in a cage.

The largest creature slowly extended his hand as if he wanted me to shake it. He dangled it in front of my eyes for quite some time.

I grabbed it. Midair we touched briefly then the creature made a quick screech and the group crawled behind the rock. Before the male could shove the ice back, I rushed past him and dozens of red eyes stared back at me in the darkness.

"Adam!" I heard Mary scream.

Caught between wanting to explore and worrying about the safety of my wife, I turned. The creature slapped the watch into my chest, pushed me back, and rolled back the boulder. That's where Mary found me, staring at what now appeared a wall of ice, clutching my timepiece.

"You found it." Mary smiled, but her face quickly dropped. "Are you alright? You look as if you've seen a ghost."

I caught my breath and nodded. "I'm fine."

She wrapped her arms about me. For a moment I forgot about finding the greatest discovery of my life. I loved the feel of her.

"I love you," she whispered.

"Do you believe in second chances and that God allows people to make U- turns?"

"Let's go," she said. "And, yes, I do."

She kissed my lips, gently. They were still freezing but I didn't mind. I didn't argue.

Chapter 26

As the plane began to lift into the sky, my heart rejoiced. For the first time in my life, I felt renewed. Protecting this species can be as rewarding as taking care of wildlife for the public.
The Yeti will probably be discovered some day, but not by me. They are smart enough to save my life, so I will return the favor.
For now let them remain a myth to the world and never know
what's become of their ancestors. That's best, after all. In the world of skyscrapers and cell phones, the Yeti can teach us all a thing or two. Suddenly, the feel of my wife's warm hand turned my eyes away from the mountains of ice below. A long road of counseling and recovery lay ahead. Living sober and keeping my family together will be worth any financial reward I could have gotten by telling the world
of the creatures.
"If I never see ice or snow again, that's fine by me," Sean grunted, in the seat across from us. "Maybe I'll sign up for my school's baseball team. Take on a warm sport."
I honestly knew Sean didn't realize how lucky he was yet to have
laid eyes on the Yeti.
"Change is good. I'm thinking of switching professions myself."
He gave me thumbs up. "No more cleaning out the lama cages on summer break. I think I've seen enough large smelly things to last me a lifetime."
Hearing him laugh, I knew we'd never be the same again. That isn't such a bad thing, after all. From this day forward hope remains our future. Like the Yeti, I'm putting my family above all else, even my own self-destructive nature.

About the Author

Michele Wallace Campanelli is an American writer, singer and Florida celebrity. During the early 1990s, Michele was lead singer of the heavy metal band, Black Widow, which was one of the first all-female bands in Florida during the early 90s. After the band, Michele Wallace Campanelli started writing short stories and fiction novels professionally. She has had nine stories appearing on the best- sellers list, including nine that reached #1 on the New York Times. Her short stories have been included in over 30 international selling anthologies. She has also penned numerous novels, magazine and newspaper articles in both fiction and non- fiction published by Simon & Schuster, Chronicle Books, Fireside Books, Fictionwise, Florida Today Newspaper, Woman's World Magazine, Adamsmedia, McGraw-Hill, Multnomah Books, Red Rock Press, HCI, America House Publishing, and Sloth Dreams Books & Publishing, LLC. Over 57 million people have read her written works internationally. When Michele isn't writing, she is CEO of Regal Entertainment Services LLC which performs concerts around Florida. She is a professional singer, writer and actor. As a devoted Christian, she uses her talents to glorify God and bring joy to others through music and her books.

No matter what your personal monsters might be, God allows U-turns. - *Michele Wallace Campanelli*